WILD ABOUT VIOLET

SARA BLACKARD

Inked Heart Press, LLC

Chapter One

-Violet-

I glance across the small coffeehouse table at my date.

Date?

Maybe.

Well, not technically, since I had agreed to just hang out with the man to help my sister's fiancé, Bjørn Rebel. But with the hunkalicious specimen seated across from me, I'm claiming this an official date, whether or not he knows it.

Seriously, though, how is it that the Rebel family is chock-full of hotties? It doesn't seem logical or fair, yet, here I am, sitting across from the most gorgeous man I've ever met, trying not to stare or drool.

Maybe both.

I sigh, then cover the childish sound by taking a long sip of the cookies-and-cream blended coffee I'm currently obsessed with. The frigid drink hits my tongue, expanding the blood vessels in my mouth and instantly rushing blood to my meninges. Sharp pain, like fire, explodes behind my eyes, and I squeeze them tight.

"Brain freeze?"

Magnus Rebel's sexy voice is all gravelly and low, like the forest fires he spends most of his time fighting have settled in his chest as smoky tones meant to lure women in. It works as it slides warmth down my spine.

Even his name is purr-worthy.

Magnus.

Maaagnusss.

I can imagine whispering it in his ear before kissing down his strong, stubbled jaw.

That is, if the first kiss works the way it should.

I shake the thought off. Thinking about kissing when we've only been here thirty minutes is not what needs to be occupying my mind. I'll just psych myself out.

"Yeah." I press my tongue to the roof of my mouth to shrink those little blood vessels back to normal. "I seem to get them a lot."

He chuckles, and I'm a goner.

When Bjørn had asked if I'd keep his brother company while Bjørn and my sister Sadie went on a search-and-rescue mission, I wasn't sure if I wanted to play host. If I didn't have to teach my art class later this afternoon, I would've totally squeezed my way on the mission. Rescuing lost souls beat keeping company with little brothers any day.

Except today.

When the little brother wasn't so little.

I'm not sure what I was expecting, but the tall, built man who'd met me outside my favorite Seward coffee shop wasn't it. Nope. I got the most pleasant shock of my life when he strolled up to me, his dark navy T-shirt stretched tightly across his shoulders and hugging his chest like a baby monkey.

What would it feel like to wrap my arms around him? Probably pretty darn good. Especially if he uses those large, muscular hands to hold me close.

He breaks a piece of his scone off and pops it in his mouth. A crumb balances on his lip before he licks it off. The temptation to lean over the table and kiss him overwhelms me, which has never happened. Trust me, with my memory, I'd know.

I sip my drink, hoping to cool off my overactive hormones. It would not look good to launch myself across the table at the poor, unsuspecting man. I may have the whole artsy persona going on, but that would be overkill.

This man is dangerous in all the good ways. I can't get my hopes up, though, not with how my dating life has been going.

"So, what's it like being a smokejumper?" I put my drink down, determined to have a normal conversation.

"Hot." But Magnus isn't helping with his wink and lopsided grin.

The giggle that bubbles out of my mouth totally infuriates me. I'm not an airhead-without-a-brain type of person. Rolling my eyes, I take another sip to focus my bouncing brain shuffling data and seemingly useless facts at me. I snag on one and regurgitate it out.

"I still find it incredible that only thirty-seven years after the Wright brothers invented the plane, men willingly jumped out of them into the middle of a raging fire." I bob my straw in my cup and shake my head. "Amazing. Can you imagine what it would've been like to be one of those first jumpers?"

Magnus shifts forward in his seat, his gaze intensely focused on me, and—oh, boy—I'm liking the effect. "Jumping has come a long way since then, but in some ways, I wish I could've been in on those first few years of it."

"Blazing trails in the firefighting world?" I wag my eyebrows at him, gaining another chuckle from him. "Did you know that in that first year the smokejumpers fought fire, they saved the government over thirty-thousand dollars? Back then, that would've been a lot."

"How do you know all this?" Magnus's voice is full of awe.

Now, to just keep it there.

I shrug, hoping to look nonchalant. "My brain just snags on to details. Plus, I went through a whole firefighting phase."

"Aw, lured in by the flames, but not willing to get burned. Few are." Magnus sits back in his chair.

"No, it wasn't that." I fiddle with my straw. "My sister was in an avalanche, but you probably already know that. Her best friend died, and Sadie would've too, if she hadn't been walking toward the door to get more wood from the porch. Made me decide that search and rescue is where I want to be."

"Not any money in that." Magnus twists his cup on the table.

"No, but it's not full-time either, so I have time to work at the kennel we all own and do my art." I pull my straw out of my cup and lick the whipped cream off.

Magnus follows the motion, his eyes dilating in the most fascinating way. So, I'm not the only one attracted.

Interesting.

He shifts in his chair, sucks in a breath, then tears his

gaze away from my lips. They tweak into a grin, but I press them into submission.

"So, you're an artist." He points to all the pieces filling the walls of the Resurrect Art Coffee Shop. "Any of these yours?"

Now, normally I'm not a showboaty kind of person. I don't paint for the accolades or the money, though both are pretty good. Colors call to me, make my fingers itch to release the abundance of thoughts jumbled in my head into something concrete. My mom used to call me spastic, but after I got diagnosed with Highly Superior Autobiographical Memory (or as I like to say, H(ey)-SAM!), they realized I was just overloaded.

Basically, I have the uncanny ability to remember every detail of my life. *EVERY* detail. The good. The bad. All replaying in my mind in technicolor wonder every day, from sunup to sundown and beyond.

Not very many people know. My parents never wanted me to have all that attention or for others to think of me differently. I totally agree, but it leaves few to talk with about it or understand what I'm going through. Art became my outlet. The way for me to process it all.

"Yeah. The three big ones back there are mine." I point my thumb over my shoulder. "I have a few others hanging around."

"Those are yours?" Magnus's chair scrapes the hardwood as he scoots it back and crosses the room.

I follow, reluctantly. Not everyone likes my style. I don't take a realism approach or even impressionism. Rather, the painting emerges in colors and emotions as I stroke onto the canvas. It's a bunch of styles of art meshed into what I call Violetism.

Normally, I don't care what others think of my art. People have all kinds of tastes. I'm not always a flavor they enjoy.

Yet, as I follow Magnus across the hardwood floor, a weight of unease settles on my shoulders. I'm putting way too much into his reaction, especially since we haven't even finished our coffees yet.

He stops and stares at the one I call *The Stormy Sea*. Dark blues and greens crash around a commercial fishing boat. I inhale, remembering the fear and adventure that piece had infused into my being. I can hear the chug of the engine as it strains against the beating waves. Can feel the frigid saltwater clinging to my skin.

"It's incredible." Magnus's softly spoken praise releases the breath I'm holding.

"Thanks." I smile at him, and he raises one eyebrow at me like I surprised him.

"Intriguing." Is he talking about me or the painting?

He runs the back of his fingers along my arm, leaving a trail of fire burning in the wake of his touch, then threads his fingers with mine. Oh, this man is trouble with a capital T.

"Tell me about the painting." He tips his chin to the boat.

The next two hours are bliss as we talk about art and fire and anything that pops into our heads. We left the coffee shop over an hour ago, after he bought *The Stormy Sea* for his sister, Astryde, who is a commercial fishing captain. We've been strolling through the Waterfront Park, talking as fishing boats motor in and out of the harbor.

I need to leave if I'm going to make it to my class on time. It's the last thing I want to do, though. Magnus is perfect: smart, adventurous, thoughtful, handsome as all get-out. I mean, who buys a sister a thousand-dollar painting because she'll love it?

Not me.

But apparently Magnus does.

He's everything I've always imagined the man I'd end up with would be. There was just one more test to prove it. My eyes dart to his lips and back to the grass in front of me. I just don't know if I want to experiment this time.

You see, I'm convinced that I'll know the man I'm supposed to be with by the first kiss. You might think I'm crazy. My sister and cousins certainly do. The thing is, everything is so vivid in my memory that if that first kiss doesn't explode within my chest with purpose, I'm confident it never will.

Before you say that's the most ridiculous thing you've ever heard, I'm here to tell you, I tested my theory out. I've kissed a lot of guys. At first, I'd kiss them several times just to make sure, but after they kept the spark to a minimum, often cooling to the heat of day-old coals, I knew my theory held.

I'll know the man I'm supposed to spend the rest of my life with when we first lock lips. Wouldn't it be amazing if that explosion happened with Magnus? I mean, it would make sense, him working with fire and all.

What would make a relationship with him even more fun is that Sadie is marrying his brother. Sadie and I will still have the same last name. The possibility makes giddiness bubble up like a pod of whales circling their prey.

"I probably should head back toward the coffee-house." I kick a spruce cone through the grass.

"You're teaching a class, right?" Magnus steps closer.

His large, callused hand feels so amazing wrapped around mine. Can I talk him into walking me back so I can have more details in the memory bank?

"Yeah."

"Maybe … I'll join? It's been a while since I took an art class."

The image of him towering over the handful of eight-year-olds bubbles a giggle out. I love my kids, but they'd roast him. Or make him model—shirtless—which wouldn't be so bad if they weren't so critical. They are dead set on being serious artists, and having some random man join them won't do.

"I don't think my students would approve." I look up at him just as my foot connects to a root.

I'm going down—arms flailing, voice shrieking down. This memory is about to go from one I want to replay every minute of every day to one that won't stop haunting me. That's the blessing and curse of being a H(ey)-SAMer.

"Whoa, there."

Magnus's strong arms wrap around my back and pull me close. I cling like a spider monkey to his neck. I'm not even feeling guilty about it, not with the way his smoky cologne fuses to my brain cells.

His hand spreads wide on my back. The pressure from his fingertips and thumb span from shoulder to shoulder in the most captivating and delicious way. It's not like I'm some petite thing, either. While effortlessly holding me up with one hand, he drags the back of his finger over my cheek, then rubs his thumb over my bottom lip.

"Violet?" His whisper is so low the breeze threatens to carry it away, but the way his gaze glues to my lips makes it very clear what he's asking.

This has to be it.

He's going to be the one.

I can feel it deep in the marrow of my bones. All fear of disappointment vanishes as I lean my lips closer. His small, happy grin might as well be a cheer of encouragement. I push to my toes, certain my search is finally over.

A hint of coffee and cinnamon gum fills my nose a second before Magnus's lips firmly capture mine. His kiss is nice, firm, yet not pushing.

It's also spark-less.

Not even an ember that might explode later.

Nada.

Rien.

Nic.

Nothing.

Chapter Two

-*KEMP*-

I ignore the giggling beside me as I troll my fifty-three-foot vessel, *Cruiser Run,* along the base of the craggy mountains jutting straight out of the ocean. The twin Caterpillar 660 hp Diesel engines hum the song of summer in my ears. It's the sound of freedom—a sound so far removed from the stress of the snowboarding slope, or, more specifically, the stress of keeping my sponsor happy, that I could listen to it for days.

Moving to Seward, Alaska and buying a fishing vessel may have been the most spontaneous plan I've ever made, but I wouldn't go back and do anything different. It's what keeps my head and heart straight. At first, getting my sponsor to agree to the summer hiatus was tough. Most athletes in my competitive level train all off-season. But I just couldn't do that anymore.

I had been on the verge of burnout and needed the off-season to not stress, to do something completely removed from the slope. In fact, though the move appeared sudden, I'd thought a lot about Alaska. Yes, there's killer snow, the World Extreme Snowboarding Championships in Valdez, and vertical runs with rollers, gullies, and wind lips that have you clenching the bum tight.

It was all that but much more.

The happiest this southern boy ever remembers being growing up is when my family took a vacation to Alaska. Dad chartered a fishing trip, and, for once, we were all laughing as Mom, Dad, and I pulled fish after fish out of the water. Of course, when we got back home, my parents' expectations hit in full force, and I eventually stopped talking to them altogether. But that one trip stuck hard in my head.

If fishing in Alaska could make my family happy, even for a little while, there had to be magic there. So when the grind of snowboarding professionally started weighing on me, my mind replayed the feel of the boat beneath my feet and the thrill of pulling in the big one in my heart, and next thing I know, I'm based out of Seward and the proud owner of the *Cruiser Run*. Thankfully, the move upped my game on the slope, so the sponsors are happy and so am I.

"So, Captain Kemp, where are you taking us now?" Stacy, the brunette who wore too few clothes for an Alaskan fishing trip, leans close … again.

She's been flirting hard the entire day, in between giggling with her cousins, that is. Her approach reminds me of the snow bunnies I steer clear of all winter. I haven't quite figured out what I'm looking for in the female department, but someone who'll hang on whichever available male they can find isn't it.

Maybe that's why paying attention to Stacy has been a low priority today. When she first arrived, I thought she was with one of the guys on the tour. Looks like she was just flirting with him too.

"There's a great spot just up the way I'm hoping will have some big fish for y'all." I point out the front window and give her and her cousins a small smile.

Most of the time, I charter older guys and families out to sea. Having a gorgeous brunette hanging on my every word is kind of nice for a change. Breaking my no-dating-customers rule isn't an option, though, so I just need to keep to my normal charm level I reserve for the tourist.

You know the one that has them having a good time with new friends.

My crew and I have become proficient at it, mainly because it's a blast seeing the excitement of our guests as they pull in big fish.

"Come over here, and I'll show you." I motion for her to step up to the helm, and I lift the side of my mouth in a grin.

Stacy simpers and closes the distance between us. She smells expensive, like the cloying scents that used to fill my parents' parlor every time my mom had friends over.

I wrinkle my nose, not liking her being so close. One thing I know for a fact that I want in a girlfriend and future wife is someone who is down to earth. I can't stomach being with someone like my parents.

Just because Stacy smells like money doesn't mean she actually has any. I learned that rather quickly in the snowboarding scene. So many people put on airs to impress.

I scan the rest of Stacy's group, looking for signs of wealth. It's there in the cut of their flannel and the sunglasses perched on their faces. No Wally World shopping for these folks. But I knew that the minute they booked the entire charter when we could fit twice as many people onboard. Could tell by the way they wrinkled their noses up at the vessel docked next to mine, laughing at what a dump it was.

What they didn't know was that "dump" made the owner a high six-figure income every year.

That's the thing I love about Alaska. No one gives a rip how much money you have or what your history is, and they definitely don't broadcast it. Some of the other captains in town are multi-millionaires, but you'd never know by looking at them.

"So, Captain, what was it you wanted to show me?" Stacy purrs the title as she rubs up against me.

I may need a spray bottle if she keeps it up.

"See the depth finder?" I point to the screen.

"Uh-huh." She's staring at me, not the dash, so I keep going with my spiel.

"Well, there's an ocean shelf that runs along this mountain. I'm taking you to where the shelf drops off. Halibut like it deep."

"Mmm, I like deep."

Ohh-kay. Hold the horses, sweetheart. I clear my throat, suddenly uncomfortable with where this conversation is going. I'm not a saint, by any means, but after a couple of bad break-ups, I decided I'd keep the family jewels stored away until I had a family of my own.

The line on the screen drops, giving me the excuse I need to leave.

"Excuse me a sec." I lean away from her, determined to go back to ignoring her.

I slow the engine and holler at my deckhands to

ready the anchor. Turning the boat so it's sitting just right in the water, I kill the engine and move to the bow to help lower the anchor. My guys don't need me there, but I *need* to be there.

Ten minutes later, lines are in the water, and my brush with the brown-haired siren is firmly behind me. If I can just get through the rest of the afternoon without having to fend her off, I'll call this trip a success. This is the last stop for the day, so hopefully the fish will bite and we can fill the rest of the limits quickly.

I lean against my seat with a sigh.

"Um, Kemp, could I get your help, please? I don't think I'm doing this right." Stacy leans around the door, her fishing pole in her hand.

Inwardly, I groan like a grizzly waking up from hibernation. The last thing I want to do is help her. But a quick glance through the windows shows that my two deck hands are busy, so outwardly I hope the look on my face is uninterested but not rude. I don't want my discomfort to cause the hands to lose their tips.

"What seems to be the problem?" I step up to the railing next to her.

"I just don't think I'm holding it right." She shrugs, completely correct.

Her rod is upside down. She's let the line run out too far, and it's not only bunching at the reel, but it's threatening to tangle with the other guests' lines. My patience runs about as thin as new ice. I really hope she didn't do this on purpose. If the lines knot up, it'll cost money and time and be an enormous hassle. I take a breath to calm down.

"Looks like you forgot to set the line." I turn the rod

in her hand and lock the reel to keep the line from going out any farther. "Go ahead and bring it in a ways."

The handle fumbles in her hand as she strains against the reel. "Why is it so hard?"

The rod tips dangerously low, like it's about to go in. I grab it so it doesn't go overboard. Stacy takes that as a cue to lean into me.

"Brace the end up against your hip and crank it, that way you don't lose the pole." I let go of the pole and step back.

She yelps and leans into me as the pole drops back toward the ocean. That thin patience of mine? Yeah, it's cracking. I realize the line is heavy with the weight needed to keep the hook near the bottom where the halibut swim, but, by the muscles flexing in Stacy's bare arms, I'm pretty sure she can handle it.

Taking the pole in my hand again, I'm about to place it in the holder mounted to the railing and clip the rod in when a beefy hand clamps on to my shoulder. I spin, coming face to face with the dude Stacy was flirting with when they first arrived on the docks. A vein is pounding on his bright red forehead.

"You think you can flirt with my girlfriend?" His fingers dig into my muscle, so I shake him off.

"Me flirting? Dude, she's been coming on to me like a possum on a persimmon." I turn back to the ocean to bring the hook in and stow the rod, my anger at the situation hot enough to boil the frigid sea. "You want your girlfriend to stop throwing herself at random guys, maybe you should figure out what you're doing wrong."

Yeah ... probably not the smartest thing to say at the moment. I mumbled it low, so hopefully he didn't hear.

Strong fingers wrap around my bicep and yank me around. Defusing this needs to happen fast.

"Man, I'm sor—" The apology isn't even out of my mouth before the guy's fist slams into my face.

I flail, trying to keep my balance without losing the pole still clutched in my hand. I'm not going to lie. That punch rang my bell, and my head swims. Just as I right myself, his fist connects with my face again.

My back hits the railing right at the spot where it lowers to the back of the boat. My momentum, and the dip in support, sends me overboard. The icy water sucks all the air from my lungs as I plunge under.

Chaos reigns on the deck as guests scream to help me out and my deckhands scramble to push through the group and throw me a line. I can't even fault the boyfriend for sending me over. It was a bonehead comment, one I would've never let out without the memory of my past tainting the situation.

A shiver shakes my body so hard it hurts. I squeeze my grip on the pole and, with my other hand, touch my eye already swelling shut. Well, at least I only lost my pride to Davy Jones's locker and not the fishing gear.

Chapter Three

I unlatch my kayak from the top of my jeep and pull my gear from the backseat. After double-checking my pack to make sure any emergency supplies we may need are there, I shove my raincoat in the top. It's surprisingly warm and sunny this evening, but if it drizzles, my sweatshirt will become a freezing death trap, as my dad, obsessed with safety, would put it.

I smile as a memory of him zipping up my lifejacket when I was twelve surfaces like a whale coming up for air, vivid as if I'm living through it again. *It's a Tuesday in early August, and we're on a family vacation to the Alaskan Interior. He wears that green plaid shirt that matches his eyes and new shoes that puts a limp to his step.*

I wrinkle my forehead and tip my head to the side. They must've given him blisters, but he never complained, not once during the week-long trip.

On the hike into the lake we are camping at, we pull wild blueberries from the bushes. I love the tang on my tongue so much that by the time we walk the mile and a half into the lake, I'm too full to eat lunch.

"There you go, sweetheart. All safe." Dad places his palm on my cheek, and I lean into the loving touch.

"Dad, I don't think the canoe will tip." I point my thumb over my shoulder at the calm lake. "It's smooth as glass out there."

"I know, but you can never be too prepared." He kisses my forehead.

Kemp's truck pulls in next to me, and the fatherly touch of Dad's kiss vanishes to the present. I smile at the blessing the memory brought. Most of the time, that's exactly what being a H(ey)-SAMer is, a blessing. Most memories that surface and play in my mind give me a boost of joy or courage or hope … whatever I need at that moment.

It's my superpower.

Kemp's door opens, and I can't help but make a dig at his tardiness. Out of the two of us, he's always prompt.

"About time you made it, Rees."

I love using Kemp's last name. Not only does it make me think of the perfect mix of chocolate and peanut butter, but it fits him perfectly. There's an entire list of history dating back to 1052 in Wales connected to that surname, but the part I like the most is the meaning: ardor, fiery warrior.

That's Kemp, all right.

He attacks life the way he attacks the slope. I think that's why we get along so well. We are both intense people; just the way we hone that intensity is different.

As he grabs his pack from the passenger seat and climbs out of the truck, I suck in a shocked breath. His left eye is dark purple and almost swollen completely shut. I grab his elbow and gently touch under the bruise.

"What happened?"

"One of my guests didn't like the fact that his girlfriend was flirting with me." Kemp winces when I skim my finger over the skin.

"No." I can't believe someone would be so mean.

"Yep." He huffs out a breath and heads to his tailgate.

"Were you flirting back?"

"Not really."

"How can you 'not really' flirt? It's either yes or no." I roll my eyes and grab my kayak from the rack.

"I pretty much ignored her most of the day. You know, the rule and all."

"Plus, she had a boyfriend."

"I had no clue they were together." Kemp shakes his head as he pulls his paddle from the back of his camper shell. "I don't know if they were fighting or what, but she hardly talked to him the entire day. Definitely didn't give a clue they were an item."

"Yikes."

"Yeah."

"So he just punched you?"

Something didn't add up.

"I may have egged him on."

"Rees, what did you do?" The smile already inches up my face.

Kemp is one of the nicest, most giving people I know. Sometimes, though, he has trouble filtering his words, especially when an injustice has been done. His lips squish to the side, and a twinkle of mischief sparkles from his one good eye.

"I may have implied that his ability to satisfy in the love department was lacking."

"No." My hands fly to my mouth as a chortle erupts at Kemp's audacity.

"Yeah. I deserved a fist to the face, but not the second one."

"Ouch." I'm trying to hold my giggles in. Really, I am, but I can imagine all kinds of things Kemp might say, and none of them are very flattering. "What did you do?"

"Well, by the time my crew hauled me out of the ocean, we'd both cooled off enough to just ignore each other the rest of the trip home."

Laughter bursts from me as an image of Kemp falling overboard fills my mind. I shouldn't find it so funny. Really, really shouldn't. Falling into Resurrection Bay is no joke.

"Not that funny, Wilde." Kemp locks his camper shell and hikes his kayak onto his head. "We going or what?"

"You're right. It's not." I grab my gear and catch up to Kemp. "Except, it kind of is."

I glance over at him, not even trying to hide my smile. His lips tweak up, and his dimple pops out. He quickly hides it with a shrug.

"How'd your date go this afternoon?" Of course, he would bring that up.

Probably because of my texts to him that Magnus should've been named Magnum for how hot he was. Is it weird that Kemp and I are so open with each other? Possibly, but for us, it works.

My happy mood fades to a ho-hum gray as the memory of that kiss with Magnus floats to the top of the others. My emotions splash over me as the memory plays in my head. Hopefulness, joy, excitement, anticipation, then extreme disappointment.

"That good, huh?" Kemp's question shakes me out of my thoughts, and I push the memory down in the ocean of thoughts always beneath me.

"Meh." I shrug and lower my kayak to the water.

"What, no lava? No molten rocks or volcanic explosions?"

"Nope. Darn shame too." I sigh as I climb in and push off the ocean floor with my paddle. "That man was hotter than a marshmallow over coals."

At least the rest of the date would be a wonderful memory. Even Magnus's lift of his eyebrow and confession that Bjørn had told him about my one-kiss philosophy would always bring a chuckle whenever the memory emerged. I'll definitely be getting back at Bjørn for spilling the beans. Not that I care Magnus knew. It's just the fact that Bjørn warned his brother or something that has my feathers ruffled.

Kemp and I paddle into the bay in silence, which is fine. I need the quiet and the salty air to soothe my soul and remind me what's really important: family, friends, and the life I love in Alaska. I spot an otter and her pup wrapped in seaweed, sleeping peacefully. It reinforces what I need to focus on.

The man I'm supposed to be with will show up someday. Until then, I'll just float on the memories of past dates and look up at the possibilities today and tomorrow bring. It's when I fight against the memories, kicking at them to stay in the depths, that I struggle.

That they threaten to drown me.

Floating is so much easier.

Be like the otter and just float.

"You know what we should do?" Kemp paddles up next to me and breaks the peace.

"Grab a Bucket of Butt at Thorn's when we get back?"

"Absolutely." He lifts his paddle toward me, and I click it in a high-five.

Maybe we should turn around now. Thorn's fried halibut is calling my name. I'm sure I hear it.

"Aside from that, we should make a pact." Kemp's paddle slices through the water with a splash.

"Another one?"

Earlier this month, we pledged to marry each other in six years, when we turn thirty, if we both haven't found the one. In a moment of desperation, with the love-enriched sounds of my sister and cousin Denali and their boyfriends floating over the fence to where I sulked on the front porch, I'd agreed. In truth, the pact had made it easier to relax about dating. Took the pressure off of me, I guess.

"This one won't be such a long-term one, but I think it'll help both of us out." Kemp points to a humpback breaching in the distance.

"Okay. What do you have in mind?" I'm only half focusing as I search for the whale to surface again.

"We need to declare a dating hiatus." His suggestion has me tipping toward him in shock.

I quickly right myself and look over at him. "What do you mean?"

"Exactly what hiatus means, Wilde." His forehead scrunches as he shakes his head at me. "We need a break, an interruption in our pursuit of happily ever after ... if that even exists."

I get Kemp's doubt in love and marriage and all that. From what he's told me, his family life isn't that great. In fact, it's so bad he hasn't talked to his parents since he left home at seventeen.

My parents, on the other hand, are the epitome of a fairytale love. They met when my dad responded to a chimney fire early one morning at a vacation rental house. My mom was there with a bunch of girlfriends on a retreat from Anchorage. According to them, it was love at first sight. He asked if he could take her to breakfast since he was getting off shift. One month later, she'd quit her job, and they'd eloped. Almost thirty years later, and they are still madly in love.

Maybe that skews my outlook on love too far in the opposite direction as Kemp's. I sigh. No maybe about it.

I'm skewed.

"So, what are you thinking?" I push my paddle through the water, relishing the strain on my back and arm muscles.

"We take the rest of the year off dating. Six months, no dates at all." His voice is firm and his southern thick. He's dead set on this deal.

"What's with you and the number six?" I joke while my mind races.

Can I take a break from dating for that long? What if the one I'm supposed to be with shows up and I miss him? Then our other pact will happen. Unless, of course, Kemp finds his one true love in the next six years.

If that happens, I'll end up alone.

"Come on, Wilde, I know you're just as fed up as I am." He splashes me with freezing water, causing me to shriek. "It's only six months."

Maybe taking a break will help. I've had a harder time keeping the memories at bay lately. They seem to want to tug on my legs and arms and pull me under.

Besides, hadn't I just said I needed to be like the otter? The reason they tangled themselves up in the seaweed is so they can rest from fishing without the ocean pulling them too far away.

Maybe my fretting over finding the one has pulled me too far from where I should be. Maybe wrapping my days with family, friends, my art, and North STAR Kennels would buoy me enough so that when I went back to hunting up a husband, I would have the energy to succeed.

I glance over at Kemp. He lifts an eyebrow in a "well?" motion. I nod, taking a deep breath as his smile stretches across his face.

"You won't regret it, Wilde." He turns back to the ocean and pushes his paddle into the water with extra force. "I can feel it in my bones that this is a good plan."

"It better be."

I hit my paddle on the surface of the water, sending a shower of water over Kemp's head. His shout startles a flock of seagulls floating next to him. The beating of their wings is like the pounding of my heart against my ribs. I'm nervous as all get-out, but I'm also more than a little relieved.

Chapter Four

-Violet-

The Rez comes into view, and I let out a sigh of relief. There aren't a lot of cars lining the street, which means a long line shouldn't delay my infusion of caffeine. I turn and smile at the most amazing human on the planet, my cousin's eleven-year-old son, Sawyer.

"Looks like we timed our arrival just right. The line won't be too long." Swerving up to the curb, I turn the key with a satisfied click.

"Wouldn't matter if there was. That would just mean more time with you." Sawyer shrugs and pushes the door open like he didn't just fill my heart with a ton of helium balloons and let them go.

Did I mention this kid is hands down my favorite person alive? Ever since my cousin Denali popped him out when she was eighteen, this kid has owned my heart. I wouldn't even need to be a H(ey)-SAMer to remember every detail of every moment with him.

I blink away the happy tears blurring my vision and rush to catch up to him. As I drape my arm across his shoulders, he wraps his around my waist and gives me a tight side hug. I lean my head down and breathe in a long pull of his unique smell, coconut shampoo with a hint of the numerous animals he keeps. I want as much detail about this memory banked for future reference.

"You done?" He peeks up at me, his eyebrow hitched in a way that's far too smug.

"One more sniff." Making a point of squeezing him extra tight, I inhale so much I go a little lightheaded.

"I love you, Vi." He giggles and slides his hand into mine. "I'm glad I'm not the only weirdo in the family."

"Hey! Being different is the bomb diggity. Just remember that." I shake his hand as we walk up the ramp to the coffeehouse.

"Well, when you have superpowers like you do, sure, but when you'd rather spend time with animals than other kids like me, not so much."

Defeat and sadness fill his voice. Is he just upset that his one and only friend is spending the summer with her family up north, or has something else happened with the mean kids in his school? My feathers ruffle, and I pull up all the names of the kids who have ever made fun of him from the depths of my memory, mentally deciding whose bike tires I need to slash first.

I may be a tad overprotective … and vindictive.

"And no one says bomb diggity anymore."

"Not true." I squeeze his hand. "I totally say it."

The soul-boosting aroma of coffee and baked goods hits me, urging me to rush inside and order, but I pull Sawyer to a stop before we cross the threshold. I am not about to let his comment slide. Caffeine and carbs can wait.

"Is everything all right, Sawyer? Why did you just

say that?" I watch his expression closely, looking for any indication he's keeping something from me.

"It's nothing."

"Hey, the most awesome person in the world does not say a sentence like that for no reason. Talk to me."

He looks away, then drops his chin to his chest with a scuff of his toe against the decking. My heart breaks into a million pieces for this kid. He has always, and I mean *always*, had superpowers of his own. He has this amazing ability to just sense how a person is feeling and adjust to their mood. I call them feelers.

If you're happy, he joins in.

Sad?

He sits next to you in silence, sharing your sorrow. Even when he was a baby, he did this. He might be more introverted in school and around those he doesn't know, but this kid has the heart of a giant and the most incredible personality.

"I just ran into some kids from school outside the Sea Life Center yesterday is all." He lifts one shoulder and takes a step forward.

I pull him back. "What did they say?"

"Nothing out of the ordinary."

"Sawyer."

"They just made a joke about me going to hang out with the only friends I have." He lifts that shoulder again. "No big deal. It's actually getting kind of old."

Why do kids have to be so mean just because someone is different? I want to hop in my Jeep and hunt down these punks. Tie them to the ground Gulliver-style and snap razor clams on all their fingers and toes.

"Violet, seriously. You don't have to go avenge me or anything." He pulls me into the coffeehouse. "I guess it just hit me harder than normal because I haven't heard from Cara in a while."

I really wish his best friend, Cara, was here for the summer instead of in the middle of the wilderness, gold mining. Those two are so tight they do practically everything together. She's the perfect ying to his yang, outgoing and spunky.

"I'm really sorry, Sawyer. More than likely it has nothing to do with you. It could be that they have issues at home, or maybe they're just mean or jealous. You know that, right?" I lean close as we stop at the end of the short line.

"Yeah, right." He totally doesn't believe me.

"Seriously. Think about it. Your dad is a pro-hockey legend. Your mom is going to be the next Alaskan reality TV star."

Sawyer snorts at that, which makes me giggle. When the Nature Channel approached us about doing a show focused on what we do at North STAR Kennels, everyone but Denali thought it was a great idea. And no, I didn't jump on the idea like it was the last lemon-lavender scone because I wanted to be a TV star. The money they offered us would help get the kennel to a more stable position. I'm even trying to figure out the best way to talk to the girls about using a good chunk of my cut to hire someone else.

I love what we've done with the kennel, and all the people we'll help with our training program for service dogs, but I want to be freer to breeze in and out when I want. I'm only twenty-four, and, as much as I love my family and Alaska, I want the opportunity to maybe see and do more. Before the TV show, I felt like leaving would be abandoning them when they needed me the most. Now, maybe my money from the show can buy me more freedom. But could I actually leave? I shake away the thought and focus back on Sawyer.

"You are like the smartest person in Seward, maybe even Alaska." I bump Sawyer with my shoulder. "*And* you're also like the best friend of one of the most famous men on television. Drew's a big deal. Why not pick on the kid who seems to have the blessed life?"

I never would have guessed that my cousin Denali would end up with *the* Drew Wilder. She'd practically closed her heart off to the possibility of love, claiming she couldn't risk Sawyer getting hurt. Then Drew showed up, and her walled heart crumbled. Not only was Drew the perfect man for orderly and tight-laced Denali, but he fell completely and utterly in love with Sawyer.

I can't blame him.

The kid is a legend.

"I guess so." He tilts his head to the side and a crease forms on his forehead.

It's like he's examining the evidence from a new angle. He's crazy smart. Since before he could talk, he was shocking us with his genius. Then, he started forming sentences, and we've been in a perpetual state of stunned awe since.

"They did seem to ramp up the verbal hits after Drew showed up." He lets out a soundless huff of a laugh through his nose, his lip kicking up on one side. "That's just silly. Drew wouldn't mind them coming out to help." Sawyer steps forward when the line moves and looks at me. "Maybe I should ask them if they want to come to the rescue sometime."

This right here is why this kid gets the best person in

the world award. He's willing to put aside his own discomfort—because he truly is more at home with animals than people, at least people his own age—and invite the kids who have been picking on him to help the superstar his mom is dating. I can't wait to see the man he's going to grow into, because the kid blows my mind away.

"Oh, great." Sawyer groans.

"What? Are they already out of cinnamon rolls?" I scan the display case, praying they haven't sold out of the ooey-gooey goodness, but cataloguing my second choice just in case.

"No. That guy in the corner is staring at you." Sawyer points, and I push his arm down.

Even though my neck and ears are getting uncomfortably hot, I chance a peek in the direction Sawyer pointed. Sure enough, there's a guy there, sipping a drink and peeking at me over the rim of the cup. He's cute too. Not as ruggedly hot as Magnus, but good-looking in a kind of nerdy way.

"Wasn't he here last time we came?" Sawyer whispers, then orders his usual.

I snap my head forward to the barista patiently waiting for me to stop ogling. After placing my order, I steer Sawyer across the room to a table by the window. If it happens to have a direct line of sight to the cute man in glasses, that is just a convenience. I chance a quick look at him as I sit, and I tuck my head with a smile when I catch him glancing over at me.

"Yeah, I'm pretty sure that guy was here before." Sawyer shakes his head. "No doubt he'll come over and start talking. Then, I'll have to waste my Vi time with watching the embarrassing display of flirting before he finally asks you out."

"You don't know that." I sit back with a roll of my eyes. "Besides, I can't go out with him now."

"Why not?" Sawyer leans forward, his eyes going wide. "Did the one-kiss rule actually work?"

Is it weird that I'm discussing my love life with an eleven-year-old? Probably. Out of all my family, he gets me the most, though. Plus, he has great instincts.

"No. It didn't work, unfortunately." I'm grumbling, I know. Guess I'm still a little peeved about No-Spark-Magnus. "Kemp and I made a pact."

"Another one?"

"Yeah. No dating for the rest of the year."

Thinking about it still makes my heart race with anxiety.

Case in point. Glasses on the other side of the coffeehouse may decide to follow his smiles over here and invite me to dinner or something. Not going may be a disaster of epic portions.

"I think that's a great idea." Sawyer drums his hands lightly on the tabletop. "You haven't been happy lately. I think taking a break will help."

Feelers, remember? Yeah, no one else but Kemp has even hinted that I might be a little more down than normal. I've been trying so hard to not show how much everything has been getting to me. I should have known I can't get anything by this kid.

"Yeah. I guess. I'm just worried, though."

"Why?"

"What if I miss my chance at finding my happily-ever-after because I say I can't go out right now?" I tip my head toward the cute guy packing up his stuff.

"What if he comes over here and he's the one and I miss it over a silly pact? I'll end up living in a one-room cabin in your backyard with ten little lap dogs and a pile of granny-square afghans no one wants or needs."

Not that I even know how to crochet.

He throws his head back and laughs. It's like water bouncing down a cliff, tumbling over rocks, and crashing with a splash into my pool of happiness. I can't be down when that sound is around. He sobers with a shake of his head.

"Vi, don't worry. If that man, or any man, is your soul mate—your one and only—it'll happen. Even if they have to wait a few months." He sets his hand over mine, a smile lifting one side of his lip though he's trying to stifle it. "Besides, if it doesn't, I'll make sure you have at least a two-bedroom cabin."

"Why, you brat." I whack his hand away as he bends forward in laughter.

"Excuse me." A deep, smooth voice like melting dark chocolate interrupts our snickering, and, oh my, the delicious sound is not what I expected to come from the man with glasses.

I swallow my laughter and smile up at him. He's much cuter close up. Blue-gray eyes, the color of the sky before a rain, dart from me to Sawyer and back. Happy crinkles line his eyes and mouth. He must smile a lot for those to be there.

"I've seen you here before. I'm Adam." He extends his hand, and I slide my much smaller one into it.

Oh, man. I love that my hand disappears in his.

"I'm Violet, and this is my cousin, Sawyer." I pull from his grip, because keeping a hold of his hand would just be odd.

Right?

Adam smiles as he shakes Sawyer's hand. His expression is filled with relief, which I guess I understand. Though I would've been pregnant at fourteen if Sawyer was my kid. Considering I've never gone past kissing, that would be difficult.

"I won't keep you, but I was wondering if maybe we can grab a coffee sometime?" Adam tucks his hand into his pocket.

Tingles swoosh from my head and land in my toes, leaving me slightly woozy. Ugh. I hate this! He seems like such a nice guy. If I tell him no, he might never ask again. Maybe I should go back on my pact with Kemp, just this once.

Sawyer lifts an eyebrow, giving me a look Denali gives him when he's trying to talk her into something she's not happy about. It's like he can read my mind, daring me to do what's right.

Fine.

I give Sawyer a glare before turning to Adam. "Gosh, I'd really like to … a lot, but I can't."

"Ah, boyfriend?" He huffs out the question.

"No," I practically shout, before I temper my answer. "No, it's just … well …" The pact seems ridiculous now as I watch this handsome man's face morph into different stages of confusion. What kind of twenty-four-year-olds make pacts like they're still in middle school? But I promised, so … "I'm taking a break from dating."

I cringe as he tips his head to the side, so I rush on.

"It sounds silly now, especially with you standing here, but my friend and I promised each other we'd not date until after the new year, and I need to keep my promise." I'm rambling, so I press my lips together to keep from saying anything more.

"I get that." Adam nods, then snorts. "Might actually be a pretty smart thing to do."

"Yeah. We'll see," I grumble as Sawyer smiles across the table at me.

Adam pulls his wallet out from his back pocket and hands me a business card. "Well, when you're taking dates again, give me a call."

"Okay." I beam up at him. "I will."

I watch him leave, then twist his card in my hand. He even has a legit job. As a graphic designer, no less. Our artistic minds could meld, and our babies could be the next Van Goghs, without the cutting off of ears, of course. Maybe I should just run out there before he gets away and tell him I changed my mind.

"I'm proud of you, Vi." Sawyer stands as our order is called out and rests his hand on my shoulder. "And don't worry. If it's meant to be, you two will enjoy that coffee in January."

"Thanks." I hug him to me, then give him a push. "Now, go get our order. I need caffeine and carbs, pronto."

He salutes, then jogs up to the counter. I slide the card into my wallet with a determined push. He's totally right. I can't be worried about what I'm missing out on during these next few months, not if I want to stay sane. Besides, it's not like a lot can happen in six months. Nothing ever happens, especially here in Seward, Alaska.

Chapter Five

-KEMP-

I can barely lift my feet as I climb the stairs to the upper dining area of Seward Brewing Company. It's like I'm wearing bunny boots filled with water. It's not the good, muscles-can't-function feeling you get after you do a killer day on the slopes.

No.

I'm dragging because at the top of these stairs my sponsors are waiting to chat. Halfway through chartering a homeschool co-op to see the sunbathing sea lions earlier, I got the call that they were in town and wanted to talk. Dread has filled me ever since, and I've been racing through my stats, publicity, anything that would warrant a trip up here to "chat about things."

They've never come up here to Alaska. Not once. And I can't come up with a logical reason for them to be here other than they're about to drop me.

I somehow make it to the top of the steps without turning around and sprinting for the truck. The president of Alley Oop, Martin, and his best friend and head of his marketing department, Rick, are laughing about something. Maybe how much of a chump I am.

Rick sees me mid-cackle and waves me over. There are two seats open at the table, so I take the one next to Rick that looks toward the ocean. If I'm about to be let go, I at least want a good view.

"Kemp, so glad you could meet us on such short notice." Martin stands and shakes my hand over the appetizers.

Normally, the smell of the Brewery's wontonachos would have me drooling. Today, the spicy cheese and beef scent curdles my already queasy stomach.

"No problem." I just have to cut to the chase. No lingering over small talk today. "What brings you all the way to Alaska?"

Rick smiles and turns his chair a little so he can face me better. Smiling is a good sign, right? Unless he wants to ease me down. Then, smiling is not the sign I want.

"We have something exciting we want to run by you." Rick rubs his hands together like a little kid getting a sundae.

I tend to hold my cards close to the chest, so to speak. After growing up with my parents, keeping my emotions and reactions hidden became a must. I think I've possibly hung out with Violet too much. It's the only explanation for me blurting out the first thing that popped into my head.

"So, you're not dropping me?"

"What?" Martin's blond eyebrows slam over his eyes. "No, man. I'd rather chop off my right arm than lose you."

All the tension from my tight muscles whoosh out in a sigh. I'm not kidding. It's an audible, shoulders-and-head-falling motion I have no control over. I've definitely been hanging out with Violet too much. Probably her entire family, since they all cover their feelings like a two-year-old playing hide-and-seek.

Okay, Kemp, focus. Stop being so dramatic, and schmooze the man.

"Well, that's a relief." I inwardly roll my eyes at my pathetic attempt at said schmoozing.

Honestly, when I'm here in Alaska, I forget all that spotlight stuff and just live. The people here don't care about the medals I've won. They couldn't give a rip about the sponsorship that pays me a high six-figure amount each year to do what I love. To them, I'm Kemp Rees, search-and-rescue volunteer, wilderness medic, and a decent fishing charter captain.

I lean back in my chair as that thought rolls through my head. Why is it I went from being under my parents' constant insistence of putting on a show to the snowboarding industry, where I'm once again on display? Why couldn't I just be happy with something as simple as what people think of me here? I love my life in Seward—the lack of stress, my friends that have become family, the small-town community—so why do I keep going away to what I don't like?

Because of the snowboarding, stupid. So, focus.

I shake myself out of it. Inner me is right. I couldn't give up the rush of snow beneath my feet, at least not now.

"I can't believe you thought we'd let you go." Rick slaps me on the back with a laugh. "The fans love you. Alley Oop's sales increasing with your face plastered on the ads proves you're a money maker, which is good for all of us."

"Welp, I'm glad I can be of service."

I push aside the icky feeling that reminds me of my parents. Being a part of the Alley Oop brand is a dream come true. Not only do I love their message to grab hold of your dreams and their program for getting kids from all walks of life on the slopes, but their products kill it. The quality and attention to detail surpasses everything else out there. Probably because both Martin and Rick used to hit the slopes competitively too.

"We've got an opportunity we want to run by you. It's too big to leave it to a phone call." Rick glances at Martin, who nods a go-ahead. "Alley Oop has been offered the chance to have a team on a TV special coming up."

"More like I badgered the heck out of the producer until she agreed." Martin's mouth hitches up on one side with a smug look. "Worked out better than both of us expected since we're now dating."

Rick rolls his eyes. "Yeah. They're disgustingly cute about it, too, which you'll realize when you meet her later." Rick shakes his head in mock disgust. "When my wife found out Martin and I were coming up here, she wheedled herself and Ivy into a trip with us."

"Which is beside the point." Martin interrupts.

"Right. The point." Rick leans closer. "Here's the deal. The Nature Channel is putting on an extreme race through the Americas. Teams of celebrities will go from one place to the next, do challenges that are both physical and mental, getting clues along the way that help them proceed to the next leg."

"Okay, I've seen races like that on TV before." Already, I'm loving the idea. They won't have to talk too long to convince me.

"Yeah, except Nature is taking all the other races, combining them into one, and making it live, like the *Hunger Games*, but without all the killing." Rick lifts his hands in front of his face and motions like a bomb exploded.

"How exactly are they going to accomplish that?"

"Because Ivy is a genius." Martin leans forward, his excitement mounting as he talks. "She figured all those other races have contestants getting to a pit stop and then leaving the following day together, but she's letting the contestants run at their own pace. There will be mandatory pit stops, but you take them whenever you get there. So, hypothetically, there should be contestants racing at all times, since it will take some a lot longer to finish."

"But what if it doesn't? Isn't that risky, having dead airtime?"

"She has contingencies for that too. She's hired commentators that will replay all the gory details if there's lag time. On top of that, every location has interviews from locals they can play if the contestants are running too close together. How she has it planned out is sheer brilliance."

Martin beams like just thinking about Ivy makes him shine brighter. He's always been an optimistic person, but the joy he's showing right now takes it to a whole new level. Being in love looks good on him. What would it be like to find someone who changes you for the better like that?

"So, what's the prize?" I can't be thinking about finding love, especially when I just made that pact with Violet.

"The winning team will get ten million dollars for

the charity of their choice and a million for each team member." Rick ticks off the prizes on his fingers. "Can you imagine how many kids we could help in our Alley Oop program? We could really ramp the winter camps up to a whole new level."

"That's an insane amount of money."

How can a network even afford something like that?

"The Nature Channel has all kinds of plans for shows coming up. They're taking their programing and kicking it up several hundred notches." Martin shakes his head and takes a drink of his beer.

"So, how big are the teams, and when does the race start?" With the excitement of the race and prize streaming adrenaline through my veins, I'm ready to get down to the details.

"Two-people teams, and the race starts in a week and a half." Rick cringes.

"That's soon." I run my hand through my hair. How am I going to pull this off? "I don't know. I have deck-hands I've hired, and two more months of summer for them. I have charters booked through the end of the season. I can't just up and leave my guys high and dry and cancel on those people."

"The race should only take about two to three weeks, and with travel before and the wrap-up after, you'll probably only be gone four weeks tops," Rick says.

"And if it was just me, I'd be all over it, but I can't do that to my guys." The sinking feeling of regret settles over my shoulders.

"What if we pay your hands while you're gone? We could even give your customers a hundred dollars as an inconvenience fee for canceling." Martin leans his elbows on the table.

Man, they really are serious about this. I want to go, more than I've wanted anything in a long time. This is a once in a lifetime chance, and these guys are making it way too easy for me to agree. It's probably selfish of me to cancel on the customers, even with the hundred bucks, but I can't pass on this opportunity.

"Well, in that case, who will I be racing with?" A smile stretches so far across my face it hurts my cheeks.

"Brittany Casing."

The name shatters all excitement, like ice dropped on pavement. There is no way on this green earth that I'll be spending any time, let alone racing around the world, with that woman. When she broke into my hotel room, thinking I'd be thrilled to find her practically naked in my bed, she'd gone too far in her pursuit. Frankly, she scares the living daylights out of me.

I never told Martin or Rick about what she did. One, it embarrassed me as all get-out. Two, on some level, I felt sorry for Brittany. Maybe not saying anything was a bad idea, but that's how I handled it.

Seems ignoring and running is how I always handle unpleasant situations. If I would have told them what was going on, I wouldn't have to backpedal about why I suddenly can't go on the race of a lifetime. Once again, I channel Violet's influence and blurt out the first thing that pops into my head.

"My fiancée won't be down with that."

Fiancée? Really? You couldn't go with girlfriend?

Yeah, girlfriend probably would have worked. Guess if I'm going to tell a tall tale, I'm going to go big. Might be the fisherman in me.

"Congratulation, man. Since when did you get

engaged?" Martin claps his hands together, probably thinking I've found an amazing love like he has.

"Yeah, I didn't even know you were dating anyone." Rick slaps me on the back again.

"It's a new development." Like, so new I don't even know her name.

"Who is she? When can we meet her?" Martin asks.

Wouldn't we both like to know?

"Her name is Violet, Violet Wilde." I'm pulling things from thin air left and right here. "She's actually going to be on a show releasing on the Nature Channel this fall about her and the dog-training kennel she owns with her sister and two cousins."

"Really? We might make this work." Rick taps his lips with his finger as he thinks. "You could race the Americas with your fiancée. and the Nature Channel couldn't argue that your team member isn't famous because they could use the opportunity to push their new show."

"Whoa, whoa, I didn't say anything about her competing with me." Even though Violet would be totally up for this. She loves adventure as much as I do. "I'll have to talk to her about this and see what she says."

Oh, and while I'm at it, see if she's game for pretending to be engaged.

"Well, if she's not your partner and you won't race with Brittany, then I don't know if we can get you in, which means we'd have to give your spot to one of the other snowboarders we sponsor." Martin stares me down, and a cold sweat slicks my back.

Would they drop me for something like this?

Whoever goes on this race will get insane exposure. It could literally change my career.

"I tell you what, let me talk to her tonight, and I'll let you know what she thinks tomorrow." Maybe I can bribe her with art supplies or an open tab at the Rez? "How long are you in town?"

"Just a couple days," Rick answers.

"Tomorrow is usually my day off from fishing, but let me see if I can talk my deckhands into coming out. I'll see if Violet can join us. It'd give you a chance to meet her and give Ivy and your wife an iconic Alaskan fishing trip."

"That sounds great, man. Thanks!" Rick turns to the server, who's picked the perfect time to ask for our orders.

Perfect, because it gives me the break I need to slow my thoughts that are tumbling like a newbie down the slope. This could work. I'll just take the next hour during dinner to formulate what exactly I need to say to convince Violet to pretend she wants to marry me.

Chapter Six

-Violet-

After mixing a little raw umber into the burnt sienna, I stroke my brush onto the canvas, adding another layer of color to Sawyer's hair. There are already two paintings propped up against the shelf drying, and, normally, that would be enough to sink the memories of the day to the depths for the moment.

Apparently, today I'm all moody and dreary. At least, according to the two paintings taunting me from the shelf. One is of Glasses (I can't think of him as an Adam). Well, it's not of him, really. No one could look at it and think, "Hey, isn't that the cute graphic designer?"

It's a painting of my hand clasped within his, but they aren't skin tone. I've painted his hand and wrist with a splendid array of oranges and yellows, my optimism and curiosity in him practically jumping from the canvas. My wrist is a variety of greens and blues. It's hope growing within my heart as I stretch out my hand to him. All this would be great. In fact, as the memory layered itself on the canvas, Sawyer's declaration that if

Adam is the one I'm meant to be with, he'll still be here in January kept playing before my eyes. Bubbles of happiness filled me with laughter as I painted.

The bubbles popped and left me stale as the colors of my hand found their way to the painting. From my wrist, the greens and blues fade to layers and layers of gray. Hope bled out to despair. Every time I tried to add more color, my mind said no, leaving me more than a little disoriented.

The next painting is of the forest from my afternoon search-and-rescue mission. A little girl had wandered off while hiking with her parents. When I'd put the canvas on the easel, I'd thought I would paint the moment we reunited the girl with her family. I love pulling moments like those up to watch them and thought I could gift the family with a painting of their joy. What I painted instead was Sitka spruce jutting up like I'm at their base looking up. There are no people, just trees, which I normally relish being within. These trees, though, bend in toward the viewer, surrounding them in a suffocating wall of color.

I couldn't stop there, not with the way my memories kept snatching at my feet, trying to pull me under to the deep today. So, I'm painting the one thing I know will leave me happy. Sawyer's head is thrown back in laughter. The sunlight filtering through the stained-glass window leaves swatches of color on his cheek and hair. I can hear his merriment. That it's not just a chuckle but comes from deep in his belly. When I'm done with this one, I'm putting it on my mantel.

A quick rap sounds on the front door, quickly followed by Kemp's voice. "Wilde, you here?"

"In the studio," I answer as I put one last stroke on

the canvas and swirl the paintbrush in the jar of water.

Studio is a loose term. Really, it's the bedroom in my one-bedroom cabin. Having a place to sleep isn't as important as having a place to paint. My twin bed set up in the living room works great for me. Besides, the only people who ever come over are family. Well … and Kemp.

"Hey," Kemp sighs the greeting as he steps into the room.

"Hey, yourself." I cringe at the bruise around his eye fading to a sickly green. That must still hurt.

Kemp crosses the room, gives me a quick side hug, then stares at the painting of Sawyer. "This is amazing. I can almost hear him laughing. It's the one that always makes me laugh with him, even if I don't know why."

My breath whooshes out with a smile. I'm glad it's not just me who sees it. Then again, Kemp seems to always get my paintings.

Which is why I swirl the brush in the jar a little too vigorously as he wanders to the paintings drying on the shelf. It's uncanny how he goes straight to those two, though there are dozens of other canvases propped up or hanging in the studio. He runs his finger along the shelf, tipping his head to one side, then to the other.

"You doing okay, Vi?" He doesn't turn until the question is all the way out.

His eyebrows draw together, making his gray eyes darker. I swear, he and Sawyer need to make a club and call it the Sees Too Much Club. I can't ever get anything past either of them.

"I'm fine. Just a little down today, I guess." I shrug it off, not wanting to drudge up what I'd finally pushed down with painting Sawyer.

I peek at the painting on the easel, and my mood instantly lifts back up. Kemp nods and shifts on his feet, a hesitation thickening the air. Odd. He's normally not like this. When he clears his throat, scratches at his five o'clock shadow, then pulls the collar of his T-shirt like it's choking him, I put the jar down.

Something's happened, and, from his nervousness, it must be big.

"Well"—he clears his throat again, his eyes looking at me before they dart away—"I think I might have news that will pick you up."

I sure hope so because the way he's acting is bundling nerves in my gut.

"Really?"

"The guys from Alley Oop are here."

"In Seward?"

I've wanted to meet them for years. The way Kemp always talks about Martin and Rick, they seem like a lot of fun. They've never come here before, though.

"Yeah. They want me to go on this crazy race through the Americas that the Nature Channel is putting on."

The tangle of nerves uncoils in an instant and transforms into springs of excitement. I bounce over to him and grab his hands.

"Oh my goodness! This is amazing." I throw my arms around his waist and give him a hug.

"It is." He pats me on the back, his voice not showing the enthusiasm it should.

"So, what's the problem?" I step back, spearing him with my you're-acting-weird look.

"The race is teams of two, and they want me to be with Brittany."

"No!"

Horror rushes from my mouth at the thought of that woman and what she put Kemp through. If I could, I'd find her and give her a talking to about appropriate flirting and that no means no. No one should have to tell someone over and over again that they aren't interested. And they definitely shouldn't have someone breaking into their room and setting up shop.

"You should've told them what she did last winter." I rub my fingers over my eyes.

"I know. I know." Kemp sighs so deep I want to give him another hug.

"What are you going to do? You can't be her partner, not in a race around the world."

"Well, I told them I couldn't be with her." Kemp chews on his bottom lip.

"What did they say when you told them why?"

"The thing is …" He paces away, tapping his hand on his leg as he walks. "The thing is I told them my fiancée wouldn't want me going around the world with another woman."

I try to hold my laugh in. Really I do, but it comes out so fast and forceful, there just wasn't any way I could.

"You told them what?"

"Yeah, I know." Kemp spears his hand through his hair as he turns to me. "It just kind of spewed out over the wontonachos, and I couldn't take it back."

"But why be engaged? Why not just say your girlfriend?"

"Who knows what the heck I was thinking in my panic?" He throws his arms wide in exasperation.

"So, what did they say?" I press my lips together to stop my mouth from the smile that wants out.

He shifts on his feet again, and holding in my amusement is difficult.

"Well, when I told them that my fiancée is one of the stars of the new Nature show starting this fall, they thought her being my teammate was a great idea." He grits his teeth in a cringe, his eyebrows almost reaching into his hairline.

"Wait. You told them I was your fiancée?" My laughter dries up.

"Yeah."

"Why?"

"Because … well … because you're my best friend and the only one I would want to race around the world with." Kemp shrugs and shoves his hands in his pockets. "Besides, I knew the two of us would dominate."

He couldn't have spoken truer words. Together, we rarely lose, no matter what the game is. But a race around the world? My toes tingle with anticipation. Yet, I'm not about to let Kemp off the hook so easily.

"True, but I can't lie. You know I can't. They'll see through us the minute we pretend to be in love."

My face always gets this weird, panicked look whenever I try to fib. Something about having lies in my memory bank leaves me itchy. It worked to my parents' benefit when I was in high school. They always knew when I was up to something I shouldn't have been.

"I know. Don't worry. I'll take care of that." How he expects to do that is beyond me.

He pulls his hand from his pocket and bends to one knee. My heart pounds painfully in my chest as he holds up the Alaskan jade ring I'd been gushing over at the Fourth of July celebration. The local jewelry designer had set the eye-shaped jade in a delicate gold band lined with small gold nuggets. Most jewelry flaunted the Alaskan treasure, but this piece had the jade front and center.

"Violet, will you agree to marry me, to trek the globe, and figure out the future when we're back on Alaskan soil?" He'd thought this through.

His words make the ruse not a lie but leaves us an out when we get home. My mouth tweaks up in amusement. What a smart, cunning friend I have. He wags the ring at me.

"You even get to keep the ring, whether or not we win the million bucks … each." He drops the amount of the prize with a lift of one eyebrow.

Excitement explodes like those color cannons used in races and gender reveals.

"Each?"

"Yep," Kemp answers, lifting the ring a little closer to me. "And, if that wasn't enough, the Nature Channel is donating ten million dollars to the non-profit of the winning team's choice. The Alley Oop guys can take the winter camps for kids to a whole new level with that kind of money."

I've loved the idea of getting kids on the slopes since Kemp first told me about it. He's promised that this winter he'll make it so I can come with him to the camp and help. I take a step closer.

"There's still the problem of us pretending we're in love."

Because we definitely are not in love, at least not beyond friends. It's not that Kemp isn't attractive. There is a reason beyond his insane skills on the slope that women throw themselves at him. It's just that ever since he's moved up here, we've been friends—best friends, really. We never ventured into the dating arena together. I cock my head at that thought. Had I been scared I'd mess up a friendship? Probably.

"I'll take care of that too. No one will guess we aren't in love."

"How are you going to do that?"

"I've been putting on a show since I was two, remember? My childhood honed me for this." He leans his arm on his knee like his hand is getting heavy. "Yes or no, Wilde?"

I take another step forward, sucking in a deep breath as the space between us closes. Agreement pushes against my lips, wanting to burst out in excitement. I swallow it down and cringe.

"I need to think about it. Can I answer you in the morning?"

My answer whooshes out on my exhale, leaving me slightly lightheaded. Kemp's shoulders slump, but he quickly covers it with a nod.

"I get it. I probably should've thought through my answer to them too." He sighs and hands me the ring as he stands.

"But I didn't say yes." I twist the ring in my fingers.

"Doesn't matter. That ring was made for you, Wilde, whether you say yes or not." He clears his throat and shifts from one foot to the next. "I'm taking Rick and Martin and their plus ones on the boat tomorrow for a fishing trip. If you decide to be engaged to me, would you want to come?"

"Sure."

Tomorrow? My skin gets cold and clammy. Do I take this opportunity for adventure, or is this the worst idea ever? This is going to be one long night.

Chapter Seven

-KEMP-

-Kemp-

I watch the depth finder, waiting for the moment the shelf drops off so I can stop the boat. So far, the day has gone amazing. Violet called at six with her yes, and all our guests have almost limited out on fish and had a blast doing it. Aside from the fact that lying makes my meager breakfast curdle in my stomach, the day couldn't get any better. I hate not telling the truth. It brings back feelings from my childhood I'd rather keep stuffed in the dark recesses of my mind.

Violet's laugh floats over the engine and rush of the wind, and I peek into the cabin. She's talking animatedly with Rick's wife and Ivy, her arms swinging wildly with whatever story she's telling. Catching me watching, she smiles up at me before continuing her story.

She's been amazing, like always. Her ability to make friends with complete strangers really blows my mind. It shouldn't surprise me, not with the way she took me in when I first moved to Seward.

"Your fiancée is great." Martin steps into the cockpit

from outside. "I can see why you'd want to snatch her up."

I inwardly cringe but paste on a smile and nod to cover my discomfort. Martin and Rick seem to love her. Maybe I should just come clean and tell the truth. It will still benefit Alley Oop and the Nature Channel, having Violet as my teammate.

"The two of you together are going to make the audience go wild." Rick shivers as he steps in out of the wind. "You being engaged is going to work out so much better than we originally thought."

Welp. Spilling the beans is a big negative. The ocean shelf drops off, and I focus on getting the boat situated and putting lines in the water.

"I'm a little nervous about having the camera on us all the time." Violet's chatting to Ivy, the show's producer. "I'm sure whatever challenges you've dreamed up will be difficult. It'll be easy to let tensions rise."

"I'm kind of banking on it." Ivy chuckles as she drops her line in. "That's what makes good television."

Violet's nervous laugh twists my heart. I'm such a selfish jerk for making her do this. I walk around the bow, heading to Violet to help her out. She shouldn't have to keep the conversation going on her own.

"Nature has a cameraman named Bo that came up and filmed our show." Violet stares at her pole, her shoulders tight with tension. "He's great. Really nice and makes a person comfortable, even with a camera permanently affixed to his shoulder. He's such a wonderful guy and cute if he ends up in a shot. I don't think I'd be as nervous if he was there."

Ivy's forehead creases as she looks at Violet, her eyes darting from Violet to me. Great. If Violet keeps going on and on about Bo, she'll blow our cover before we even leave home. I've got to fix this, stop her from talking us out of the race.

Her line bobs, and she freezes. Maybe the Man Upstairs is helping me out by sending a halibut to distract the conversation. Then again, helping someone lie probably isn't something He'd do.

She reaches for her line and feels the length for tugging. My lungs expand with a satisfied breath. Only someone raised next to the sea would be this calm. I shake my head at her confident smile as she reels in her line.

"You caught one already?" Ivy gasps, her eyes widening.

"Well, when you have the best captain in Seward, it's easy." Violet shoots me a smile.

Okay, maybe all is not lost. Now, we just need to keep it up and erase any doubt Ivy has. Violet whoops as the pole tugs against her hands and line races out.

"Oh my gosh." Her muscles strain as she pulls up on the pole. "It's a big one."

I come up behind her, hovering my hand under the pole just in case she needs help.

"Let's get Ivy's line out of the water so Vi can move to the back of the boat," I holler at my deckhands.

We'll have more room to get the fish out of the water at the open stern. Violet's reeling already lags. When she strains to lift on the pole, I wrap my hand around hers and help as we stumble along the railing to the back.

"You've got this, babe."

I startle at how easily the endearment slips off my tongue. My brain freezes, suddenly crashing like my board caught the edge wrong. I don't even think Violet heard me, but it's odd how right it sounds. Shaking my head, I laugh at myself and focus on getting the fish in.

"Rees, I can't." She grunts as she struggles to pull the pole up.

"You can. We do this together."

I brace my front against her back. Wrapping my left hand around the pole, I help her lift it so the tip is at eye level. My muscles strain against the weight. This fish is a beast.

"Quick. Reel, reel, reel, reel, reel," I urge her as we let the pole down.

Not that she needs the prompting. She's been fishing these waters since she was little. When the rod is perpendicular to the water, we lift without me saying a thing.

For thirty minutes, we repeat the cycle of lifting and reeling. Both of us heave to catch our breaths. Violet groans with each spin of the handle.

"Kemp!" She gasps, her arms shaking against mine.

"I know, babe. I know, but you've got this, honey." Wow. I'm just throwing nicknames left and right.

"I see color," one of my deckhands yells.

"Holy moly. It's huge!" Martin's impressed, so I peek at the water.

My eyes bulge at the amount of white belly swimming there.

"Vi, you may have won this year's halibut tournament," I say as I grit my teeth and pull when the halibut gets extra feisty.

"I'm done, please. Let's just get it out of the water." Violet's voice trembles, and I squeeze her with my arms.

"Okay. You pull. I'll reel." I slip my hand under hers on the crank.

She nods, grabbing the pole with renewed strength. Two more cycles and the fish is close enough to snag. My two deckhands hook the monster and, with grunts and a roar, yank it from the water. I hand Martin the pole as Violet slumps against me.

"You did it." I pull her into a hug, rubbing my hands down her shaking arms.

"No. We did it." She looks up at me with the most beautiful smile, and I'm tempted for the first time in our friendship to bend down and kiss it. "I'm going to be sore for a week."

Chuckling, I push the troubling thought of kissing her aside and pull her toward the halibut. Ivy films us with a small camera she brought. Did she buy the whole engaged bit? Was she still questioning Violet's words about Bo? I press my lips to Violet's hair and give her another squeeze, just in case the show we just gave wasn't enough.

Chapter Eight

-*Violet*-

As I slice the filet free from the side of the halibut, I glance to the end of the dock where Martin, Rick, Ivy, and Candy stand talking. They haven't stopped chatting, their heads all bent in together, since Kemp and I pulled in the halibut. I honestly don't know what to think. Ivy peeks over at me, then ducks her head back into the huddle.

Sighing, I go back to butchering the halibut. This is going to take a while. Thank goodness the town built the cleaning stations here on the docks. I wouldn't want to mess with this monster in my house. I'm halfway through when my dad steps up beside me. His low whistle tugs a smile through my exhaustion.

"Hey, sugar. Kemp said you got a big one, but that was an understatement." Pride always flows so freely through Dad's voice, even when he's exasperated with me and my sister, Sadie.

"One hundred sixty-two pounds." I set the knife down. My arms are so sore I can hardly lift them.

"Oh, honey. That might be the year's record." Mom claps, her face beaming from the other side of Dad.

"Yep. We'll have to have a halibut fry to celebrate." I can't hold in my yawn.

"You go on home, sugar. Kemp said you put up a long fight and are exhausted. We'll take care of this." Dad pulls me into a bear hug.

"But—"

"No buts, Vi. Your Uncle Joe is on his way to help." Mom gets in on the hug, encasing me with parental love I just sink into. "You head on home, take a nice long bath, and relax."

"Well, if you're sure."

They give me another squeeze. This moment right here is the best memory of the day. Much more fulfilling than bagging the biggest halibut ever.

I turn to wave goodbye to Kemp's sponsor, but they're even more engrossed in their talking. Kemp disappeared when we docked, probably because he's upset that I couldn't pull off the charade. I'm just done, ready to be home and wallow.

I mean, I can't even fake date correctly.

Maybe I just need to take mine and Kemp's hiatus on relationships and extend it indefinitely. I trudge off the pier, ready to take Mom's advice and soak in a hot bath while eating the rest of the brownies stocked in my cupboard. Tomorrow's going to be another long day painting a mural at Drew Wilder's animal rescue center. I groan just thinking about lifting the paint brush.

"Wilde, wait up," Kemp calls just as I walk into the alley between the tall buildings lining the pier.

I don't think my shoulders have ever heaved as much as they do with my sigh. I'm not ready for what I'm sure he's going to tell me. Despite having to lie and pretend, I was really looking forward to the race.

"Sorry, I got cornered by Captain Lee." He glances over his shoulder at where my parents are and back, his forehead creasing in concern. "You heading home?"

"Yeah. I'm tired, and tomorrow's going to be busy."

"Right. The mural. Can't wait to help."

He pushes his hands into his pockets and rocks back on his heels. I hate that there's this awkwardness between us. What's going to happen when we get on the race? *If* we get on the race. Will the unease thicken? Will our friendship change? I should've thought about that before I agreed to this ploy. Movement catches my eye, and I peek around Kemp to see his visitors leaving the pier.

"I don't think they bought it." I don't look at Kemp as I speak because I don't want to see his disappointment.

"You don't know that." He shrugs. "I think we did a pretty good job. It's not like we have to be sucking face to prove we're engaged."

I bite the inside of my cheek and twirl the fake engagement ring on my finger. What if we have to kiss? I've had my one-kiss rule for so long, I don't know if I can break it, especially if we have to multiple times. Memories of one-time kisses are easy to push to the depths. It's the multiple ones that bob to the surface when I least expect them, clinging to me with their tentacles of discouragement and heartbreak and pulling me under. It's hard for me to float over the memories with them taunting me, telling me I'll never find that special someone who understands me or accepts me.

They don't surface much, not anymore. But when they do, they slick over me, making it hard to break free. I don't want to deal with them while we're racing around the world, but I can't tell Kemp that. I need his friendship too much to risk telling him about my hyperthymesia. The few times I have told people, it's come back to bite me in the backside.

I don't want to ruin this opportunity for us either, though. Maybe there's a way to look like we're madly in love without actually kissing. Kemp's visitors walk closer, so I grab the front of Kemp's shirt and pull him farther into the alley.

"Wilde?"

Stopping a few feet in so we're not out in the open but not completely hidden, I push to my toes and whisper in his ear, "Just play along."

I spear my fingers through his hair. It's soft against my skin. He tentatively puts his hands on my waist, his palms barely touching me.

Peeking to the pier, I watch Martin look left and right as Ivy, Rick, and Candy lean over Ivy's phone. Martin spots us, and I snap my eyes away. Show time.

"You're gonna have to do better than that, Rees," I say as I pretend to kiss down and back up Kemp's neck.

My lips brush his skin as I talk, and he sucks in a breath. My heart pounds hard twice against my ribs before he pulls me tight against him. I swallow at how amazing his large hands feel spread across my back, like he could hold me up forever.

"Good. They're almost here." My mouth grazes his ear as I try my best to angle my head so it looks like I'm kissing him without actually kissing him.

This display had better work. I wrap my arms more tightly around Kemp's neck. He stumbles forward, catching our fall into the siding of the building with one hand, while making sure I don't crash into the hard surface with the other. His forehead bangs into the wall with a loud thunk.

"Ow." He leans against me, and I stifle a laugh as I look up into his face.

His eyes squeeze closed.

"You okay?" I half laugh, half whisper.

"Yeah." He opens his eyes and grins down at me.

Both of us barely hold in our chuckles as we stare at each other. His presence still presses me against the building. He leans forward, angling his head along mine, and a shiver races down my back. What the heck?

"Aside from me bashing my head into the wall, that was convincing." His breath against my neck makes me giggle.

"Kemp," Martin hollers. "Oh, sorry."

We straighten from the siding and turn to Martin. Kemp drapes his arm across my shoulder like he has a hundred times before, but it feels different now. More weighty.

"Thanks for the fun day, guys." Martin points his thumb over his shoulder at the three still arguing over Ivy's phone. "We're going to squeeze in some more sightseeing before we leave. I'll let you know if the network is going to let you two be a team as soon as I can. It was really nice meeting you, Violet. Keep this guy in line for us."

I nod, glad at least the pretending for today is done.

As the group waves their goodbyes, Kemp speaks low in my ear. "See. Together, we've got this."

I sure hope we do. I lean into Kemp as he walks me to my car. If future days go anything like today did, pretending to be Kemp's fiancée will mean being constantly on guard with what I say and do. I've always had a hard time with that.

Chapter Nine

-*Violet*-

I stare at the side of Drew's animal rescue center, comparing all the sections of the mural with my mock-up to make sure I've labeled everything correctly. Everyone should be here any moment, and I mean everyone.

Denali and Sawyer would have been here anyway because of Drew. So would Drew's mom, Stella. I hadn't expected my sister Sadie and her boyfriend Bjørn to volunteer. Nor my cousin Rory, especially with how she's more of an indoorsy kind of gal. I guess it makes sense her best friend and local vet, Mark, wanted to help. He's excited for Drew to get the clinic open. Plus, he's not-so-secretly in love with Rory, though she's the only one who hasn't clued in. Even my parents and aunt and uncle are coming for a bit.

I need to make sure my setup is perfect. Once Denali and Sawyer got excited about helping, everyone else jumped on board. Since I normally paint the murals on my own, at a pace I pick, stressed is an understatement. It'll be fun, a memory to cherish, but I'm paranoid I'll forget a step and ruin the mural.

This painting might be one of my favorite murals so far. I love the animals hiding in the woods and grass, the bright colors, and how I've lined the painting so the horizon is a continuation of the landscape past the building. It'll be the first thing people see as they pull into the grounds, so it has to be perfect.

Tires crunch on the gravel, and I tuck my mock-up into my pocket so I don't set it down somewhere and lose it. Sawyer jumps out of the vehicle before Denali stops completely. She shakes her head and waves through the windshield.

"Good morning." Sawyer runs up to me and throws his arms around my waist.

"Best greeting ever," I say, squeezing him closer and taking a hit of his coconut scent.

"You smelling me again?"

His chuckle erases all my stress. Even if the painting isn't perfect or I have to come back and fix it, having everyone here to help will be worth it.

"Yep. Not even hiding it."

I ruffle his hair, draping my arm across his shoulders as we turn to his mom. She's carrying four bags from the Rez, and I drool. In my rush to get over here and set up, I forgot to eat breakfast.

"I don't care what you have in those bags. I'm going to need two, maybe three, of them." I grab the one she's holding under her chin and set it on the closest of the tables dotting the yard.

"There are coffees in the car. Why don't you and Sawyer go get them?" Denali drops the rest of the pastries on the table and sags against it.

"You brought coffee too?" I throw my arms around her waist and smack a loud kiss on her cheek. "You're an angel, a saint, the goddess of starving, uncaffeinated artists."

"Ew, okay. Geesh, laying it on thick much?" Denali pushes me away with a chuckle.

"It's true, you know. The whole goddess bit." Drew's Australian-accent fills the air as he saunters around the front of the building, his eyes trained on Denali. His hair is wet, like he just got out of the shower, and a smile slowly builds the closer he gets. "Though she's more of the siren variety with how she lures me in."

He trails the back of his fingers along her cheek before burying them into her hair. Denali's blush is adorable, and one I haven't seen enough of over the years. Drew leans down and softly touches her mouth.

"Good morning, love," Drew whispers against her lips.

"Talk about ew," Sawyer grouses, but his wide smile counters his words.

"I think it's cute." I push Sawyer's shoulder.

Denali's blush deepens, and she lifts her eyebrow at us. "Aren't you two supposed to be doing something?"

"You mean besides gawking at you, kissing the world's sexiest man alive?" I wag my eyebrows at her.

"Crikey, Vi, that was like three years ago." Drew shakes his head. "You can't keep calling me that."

"Oh no," I reply, my voice dead serious. "That's not a throne you get thrown from, buddy. You'll forever hold that title. I even had buttons made."

"Are you serious?" Drew's forehead creases as he looks down at Denali. "Is she serious?"

"Well, it is a lifetime deal." Denali pats his chest. "One I certainly agree with."

"But ... buttons?" Drew stutters.

Denali kisses him on the cheek. "You'll get used to it."

I drape my arm across Sawyer's shoulders and lead him to get the coffees. "Wonder what he'll say when he sees the bumper stickers and T-shirts I ordered too."

We both peek back at them. Drew's expression is the epitome of worry, all wrinkled brow, his hand rubbing down his face. Denali pats his chest and kisses him more deeply.

"He's gonna freak." Sawyer giggles, then we both crack up laughing.

Being a part of our family means you have to stay on your toes. Drew is an only child from only-children parents. He's never had cousins or siblings to give him a hard time. As our family's live-free-and-wild child, I think it's only right that I welcome him in big style ... or scare him off. Though, I think it'll take a lot more than clothing and stickers to turn Drew away from Denali.

Three hours and several pastries later, the mural's layers emerge more with each pass of the brush. While I study everything we've done so far, I lean back against the picnic table and sip on the lemonade Drew's mom, Stella, made for everyone. The lady is obsessed with lemons. Claims she doesn't want us all to get scurvy living up here in the wild north. She's also obsessed with art, which has been helpful today. She's been the extra eyes I didn't realize I'd need.

Truth is I'm a bit off. When Kemp showed up, he still hadn't heard whether or not we are a go for the race. I've been trying not to let that bother me, but it does. Alley Oop's determination to have a team on the race worries me. If the Nature Channel says no, will they make Kemp race with that horrible woman? Will they pick someone else entirely? It didn't seem like they'd drop Kemp's sponsorship altogether, but I don't know enough about how contracts work to know for sure. I should ask Kemp if that's a possibility next time we can't be overheard.

"Oh, shoot." Kemp trips over the hose and fumbles with the brush and cup of paint in his hands.

Bright pinkish-purple paint for the fireweed splashes down his shirt and all over his hands.

"Again?" Bjørn calls out. "Man, you didn't take your anti-clumsy pills today or what?"

"Something like that." Kemp sets the cup and paint on the grass just as his phone rings in his pocket. "Great. It's my sponsor."

My ribs cinch up like that one time I wore a corset for theater. Except I vowed to never wear one again, and this tight sensation suffocates more painfully.

"Here. Let me help." Sawyer plucks Kemp's phone from his back pocket and hits the speaker button.

"Hey, Martin. You leave yet?" Kemp's eyes dart to me.

"Just now. I wanted to call before we took off and let you know that the Nature Channel agreed to the switch in teammates." Martin's words propel me from the table and across the yard.

"Really?" Kemp pumps both fists in celebration and throws me two thumbs up.

Everyone has stopped painting and is listening. Hopefully, we can explain about the race without letting them know about the whole fake engagement. I peek at my parents, who just showed up to help. I don't think they'd be too understanding.

"Yep. I have plane tickets for you and Violet. You leave next Wednesday." Martin's excitement blares through the speaker.

"Awesome. Thanks!" Kemp wags his eyebrows at me.

I try to motion to him to get off the call before it reveals too much. I do the international hand motion for hang up. You know, the one with your pinkie and thumb flipping onto one of those ancient telephones my parents grew up with. Kemp just keeps smiling at me like a loon, paint still dripping from his hands.

"Tell that fiancée of yours she's incredible." Martin's words stop me in my tracks like a lynx caught in the headlights. "Anyone other than Violet, and I don't think the network would've gone for it. She's pretty amazing."

"Yep. Yep, she is." Kemp swallows and shifts on his feet.

"The flight attendant is giving me the stink eye. I'll send you the information." Martin hangs up without saying goodbye.

Not that it really mattered. Not with the way everyone's heads swivel back and forth between me and Kemp, like a bunch of owls. That imaginary corset cinching my ribs? Yeah. One look at my dad and that thing closes so tightly I can't even take a breath.

"Explain." Dad's one word rumbles into the air like a grizzly huffing his upset.

"Well, sir … it's, well …" Kemp stammers, doing a horrible job of fulfilling Dad's command.

"The Nature Channel is doing this extreme race through the Americas with different celebrity teams."

My words don't squeak out much better than Kemp's, so I clear my throat when Dad crosses his arms and raises one eyebrow. "Kemp's sponsor got Kemp in the race, which is amazing since the winners get to donate ten million dollars to the charity of their choice. Can you imagine how many kids Alley Oop could help in their winter snowboarding camps with that amount of money?"

I'm rambling. I know, but I just can't seem to stop the flood of words coming from my mouth.

"That doesn't explain the whole fiancée part." Dad taps his foot in impatience, and Mom sets her hand on his forearm.

"The engagement isn't real, so don't worry." Kemp really has no clue how to defuse this situation.

Dad's arms drop to his sides. "That's supposed to make me feel better?"

"What Kemp is trying to explain and failing, miserably, I might add, is that when Martin told Kemp about the race, he was supposed to race with another snowboarder named Brittany." I step up next to Kemp and hand him a rag to clean up his hands. "The only problem is that Brittany pretty much stalked him all last season."

"Creeped me the heck out all winter, but the worst was when she broke into my hotel room to wait for me." Kemp shivers.

"You didn't tell your sponsor?" Drew asks, and I realize everyone has inched in to listen.

Kemp pushes his hand through his hair, making it stand up on end with pink paint. "No, man. I was embarrassed and just kind of hoped that after I made it very clear I wasn't interested, she'd move on. But there's no way I can race around the world with her."

"Son, you still haven't told us how your sponsor thinks you're engaged to my baby girl." Dad has that tone he always gets when he knows me or Sadie have done something wrong and he's making us sweat it out.

"Truth is I panicked and blurted out that my fiancée wouldn't want me racing with another woman. Then it just kind of snowballed from there." Kemp's shoulders slump. "I know. It's ridiculous. I mean, who does that?"

"Lots of people, if Rory's books she writes are based on reality." Sawyer shrugs, his forehead scrunching in confusion as he washes out a brush. He's been the only one still working during this entire encounter, which, in any other circumstance, would have me laughing. "Of course, there are all kinds of other situations in her books that seem farfetched but work out."

"What are you talking about?" Denali chuckles, bumping Sawyer's shoulder. "Rory hasn't written since high school, and definitely not books."

"Sure, she has. She's written tons of books as Bristol North." Sawyer looks up now, those creases in his forehead getting deeper. "You guys didn't know that?"

Everyone's focus shifts to Rory like we're all puppets and our strings have just been pulled. Her cheeks must be roasting. I've never seen her face so red.

"*You're* Bristol North?" I can't believe my favorite author is my cousin, and she didn't tell me! "What in the world, Rory? This is huge. You're … you're famous. How could you keep this a secret?"

She lifts one shoulder and pushes her glasses up. "At first, I was embarrassed. Then, I just didn't want everyone to know." She turns to Sawyer and glares. "Still don't."

"Sorry." He cringes. "It was just so obvious I thought everyone knew, and so it wasn't a big deal."

"It's okay." Rory crosses to Sawyer and pulls him into a hug. "I guess I don't really need to keep it a secret anymore."

"What kind of books are we talking about?" Mark is zeroed in on Rory, hurt radiating from his eyes.

"The most amazing romance books ever!" I can't help but gush.

Rory's novels really are great. So full of fast-paced adventure and swoony romance. I turn to Aunt Suzie when her groan hits my ears.

"Romance, really?" Suzie teaches literature at the Kenai Peninsula College and is somewhat of a fiction snob. "I knew you letting her read *Sweet Valley High* books during middle school would bite us in the backside." She whacks Uncle Joe on the arm.

"Suz, come on. Rory's books truly are incredible." I've never understood the whole romance-is-less-than argument. I've read some really boring books that were hyped up. Romance is just as emotionally engaging as any other genre.

At least this news has gotten the heat off mine and Kemp's fake engagement. Maybe by the time everyone calms down, our predicament won't seem so bad.

"Rory, we're all proud of you. I've known you were an amazing author since you were in elementary school." Dad smiles at Rory proudly, then turns to Kemp and me, his smile fading. "But we still haven't gotten the entire story from Kemp and Violet."

"There really isn't much more to tell." I put my best

no-big-deal face on, even though sweat pools on my lower back. "Kemp and I are going to be racing around the world together. It's an incredible opportunity, Dad, one we both don't want to miss out on."

"But you're only going because of a lie."

"Not true. Kemp knows I'm a horrible liar. Our engagement is real. When we get back, we'll break off the engagement, and life will go back to normal." I think I pull off the nonchalance I was going for.

Sawyer snorts, his head shaking in amusement. "Fake relationships never go back to normal. At least, not in Rory's books."

My bravado drops a little. He's right, of course. I glance at Kemp, his head shaking in disagreement before he winks at me. But what Sawyer isn't right about is all those books have one thing in common. Usually, one or both of the people secretly love each other. Neither Kemp nor I do. We're just really good friends, and, because of that, this plan will work. It must.

<h1 style="text-align:center">Chapter Ten</h1>

I stare at the gear I have laid out on the bed. We aren't allowed to take much with us, so packing should be easy. Yet, the search-and-rescue member in me wants to be prepared for any circumstance, and I've been bouncing back and forth between what gear I should take, packing and repacking more times than I care to admit.

A knock on the front door blessedly pulls me from my debate between whether the pack of toilet paper or the wipes is the better option. I hope Violet is having an easier time getting ready for our departure tomorrow than I am. These few days have been a whirlwind of preparation, but she's been her usual, cheerful self through it all.

I open the door to find Violet's dad, Will, filling the space. The man is tall and built like the lumberjack on those paper towel commercials or an older version of Thor. His years at the fire department have kept him strong, and the look he gives me has me wondering if I should slam the door and pretend I'm not here. It's the look he reserves for search-and-rescue crew members who disobey orders. I've never had it pierce my soul, and I'm left cold and shaky from it.

"Can we talk?" Will asks, but the tone of his voice says it wasn't a question.

I swallow, the spit barely making it down my throat. Will has been clear from the start that he doesn't like this idea, but Violet promised she talked him down from casting lightning bolts. Him being here can't be good.

"Sure. I'm just packing." I motion him in and head to the kitchen. My throat is bone dry, and maybe a glass of water will get it working again. "Want a drink?"

"No. What I want is for you to call this off. Either tell your sponsors the truth or tell Violet she can't go." Will stops on the opposite side of the island, and I'm glad for the barrier.

Not that it would help me if he went berserk on me. He might, especially when I tell him no. I've thought over and over again about how to get us out of this tangle, but after the call I got last night, it's pointless.

"Sorry, but I can't do that, not with how excited the Nature Channel is about Violet." I set the glass on the counter with a loud clink. "I got a call from Martin last night, and the Nature Channel already has increased their exposure to the show for the kennel. They've woven it in with the promos they are doing to hype up the race. Changing now would hurt the work Vi and everyone have done for the kennel. I can't do that."

Will growls and crosses his arms. "Maybe not, but you can come clean about you not really being engaged."

"Can't do that, either. Not without giving the network a poor impression of Violet."

"She won't be able to do it. She's a horrible liar."

"Have you seen the commercials?" I ask, then continue when he shakes his head. "I don't think it'll be a problem."

I pull up the text from Martin, click on one commercial he sent over, and hand my phone to Will. It's a promo for the race with video from my snowboarding, Violet's bits on her show, and an incredibly convincing clip of me and her reeling in the halibut. Violet looks incredible, absolutely stunning, though she's in her bright orange fishing bibs with her hair in those silly buns she sometimes wears. Her focus and joy are magnetizing, and I have no doubt that she'll draw viewers in.

What is surprising is the look of complete adoration on my face. I had to watch it five times just to come to grips with what I saw there. If Violet just continues to be her amazing self, I'll apparently be all that's needed to have people believing we're in love. I snatch up the glass and gulp half of it down.

"I'm worried about Violet. About how she'll handle all of this." Will's low, strained voice pulls something in me, and I'm not sure how to label it.

"She loves adventure. This race is right up her alley."

"It's not the race. It's everything else—what people will think of her, the engagement scheme, the media, the other competitors—all of it." He sucks in a deep, shuddering breath.

I press my mouth shut tight to keep the protests from spewing out. Sure, Violet is different, but it's her uniqueness that draws people in. Will's just being an overprotective dad, and, in some ways, I'm envious of Violet for having someone who worries over her like that.

"I won't let anything happen to her, Will. You know I'd never want Violet or any of you to get hurt. You're the closest thing I have to family." My voice cracks, and I turn to look out the window.

Since I first showed up, the Wildes have taken me in, made me one of them. Holidays, birthdays, weekend camping trips … all of it, they've just slid me right in with them. I've never, not in all my life, felt as at home as I do with them. So, Will's lack of faith in me bites.

"Violet—" Will shakes his head and drops his chin to his chest with a sigh. "Violet processes things differently than others."

What in the world does that mean? The way Will puts it sounds … I don't know, bad. I fist my fingers. He might be her dad, but he shouldn't put Violet down. I relax my hands, shoving them in my pockets so I don't do something stupid like dive across the island and deck Will.

"Violet is the most amazing person I know." So, I couldn't keep the anger out of my voice, and the way Will's head just popped up, I think he heard it. "Out of everyone I ever met, she's more equipped than anyone to handle this."

"Kemp, it's not that simple."

"What isn't?"

"She's got … issues that … that will make this hard, especially the social part of it."

Will isn't making a lick of sense. What issues could she possibly suffer from?

"What are they, and I'll make sure to help her. Protect her."

"I …" Will takes a step back. "It's not for me to tell."

The hair on the back of my neck stands at attention. Now, all kinds of worry for Violet flock into my brain like those seagulls from *Finding Nemo*. I go with the biggest and loudest one squawking.

"Is she sick?" The water I just downed rolls in my gut.

"No. No." Will's eyebrows crease together, and he raises his hand to stop my train of thought. "Nothing like that. I really shouldn't have said anything. Just promise me … promise me you'll be there for her, especially when this whole charade you have going on gets difficult."

"I will always be there for Violet. Always."

I mean it too. No matter what this life brings, whether on the race or after, I will never let Violet Wilde down. She's the only one who has ever made me feel at peace with being myself. The only true friend I've ever had. Disappointing her isn't an option … ever.

Chapter Eleven

-Violet-

I probably look like the biggest loon, but I can't help the smile stretched across my face as we board the plane and find our first-class seats. Martin insisted he pay for us to fly in style, and I didn't argue for one second. I'm imagining caviar and mimosas. Or … maybe just sparkling cider since I've never enjoyed drinking. Whatever. It's going to be amazing.

Plus, it'll be perfect. Kemp and I have had no time to talk about how we want to play the whole engaged bit. It's been a hectic few days getting ready to leave with a few search-and-rescue missions thrown into the chaos. I'd sacrifice the perfect packing for saving people any day. But that leaves us with just the hours on the flights to Washington D.C. to make sure we know for sure how we'll answer questions that come up. If we are going to make this work, I'm not wasting any of them.

Kemp grabs my backpack and hoists it up into the overhead bin. "Tone it down, sunshine. If you're gonna

"

sit in first class, you need an air of snobbery. Or at least, not beaming to the world you're a newbie."

He's teasing, of course. I haven't stopped asking him questions since we sat in the Alaska Lounge munching on the fully-stocked buffet. He's used to flying first class, where I'm usually somewhere in the back half of the plane, thanks to Dad's insistent frugality.

"Oh, I'm beaming all right. Good thing I took the aisle seat. I may even stop people as they walk by to let them know how excited I am." I jiggle my shoulders in a small dance.

"You wouldn't."

Kemp isn't the most demonstrative in public. He puts on a good show on the slopes and is incredibly supportive of other snowboarders both in front of the cameras and off, which endears him to the public. It's why he didn't out Brittany's stalking. Yet, he's always one to keep life low-key when he's away from all the attention, even though he's one of the most amazing athletes competing at the moment. So, me doing something like that would kill him.

"Maybe."

Kemp rolls his eyes and slumps into his seat. There's a smile playing on his lips, so his pout-fest is all for show. I think.

I slide into the chair, letting the size and comfort surround me. "This is so much better than coach."

"Really?"

I turn to him, searching his face for a jest. "You've never flown coach?"

"No. I don't think so." He shrugs, like it's no big deal he's always flown how few fly.

"How is that even possible?"

Do I want to know? Kemp has always been quiet about his past. I know he doesn't get along with his parents and that they are well off, but that's about all I've got. I figured if I'm willing to keep my H-SAM from him, he could keep his past from me. It didn't change who he was or our friendship.

"Well, growing up, we always took our jet. Then, when I left, I was already sponsored. They bought my tickets to most places." He fiddles with the literature in the seat back and talks without glancing at me.

Private jet? His parents are richer than I thought.

"Yeah, but what about when you come home? Your sponsors don't pay for all your travel."

It has to be a lot more to fly up here, otherwise everyone would do it.

"Wilde, why would I sit back there, scrunched between people I don't know, with no leg room to stretch out when I can afford to sit up here the few times I have to buy tickets myself?" He sits back and gives me that look like I'm not thinking straight.

"Yeah, but—"

"Trust me. After flying up here, you won't ever want to go to coach again."

"That's what I'm worried about."

I peek back at the rows and rows of seats crammed into the cabin. Families already sit in some. A baby cries, and we haven't even taken off. I huff and turn forward. Kemp pats my hand before he digs through his backpack at his feet and pulls out his headphones.

"Oh, no you don't." I snag his headphones and put them back in his bag.

"What?"

"I told you, we need to get our story straight."

I turn sideways in the seat so I don't have to kink my neck and tuck my leg under me. Oh, man. These seats are amazing. I'd never be able to do this in coach.

"What's to get straight? I asked you to marry me and you said yes. End of story." He reaches for his bag, and I swat his hand.

"Seriously?"

He lifts both hands in question. "Uh … yeah. What more do you need?"

I roll my eyes and shake my head. "No wonder you don't have a girlfriend."

"Hey, now. I do just fine with the women. No need to hit below the belt." He crosses his arms over his chest and leans against the wall … away from me.

Guilt coats my tongue like fireweed fluff. He's touchy about his lack of dating, especially lately. It's something we've groused about often together. It's why we made the two pacts we did. I really shouldn't have sunk that low.

"Okay. Sorry." I swallow, not wanting our trip to start off bad. "Forgive me, please?"

I drag out the end of the word, smiling wide with all teeth showing while I wrap my fingers around his arms. He huffs a laugh and shakes his head.

"Fine. You're forgiven." His gaze darts behind me, and he quickly uncrosses his arms and grabs my hand closest to him. "I'll always forgive you, even when you're an imp."

He tucks my arm beneath his and threads his fingers through mine. It's warm—comforting—like a cinnamon roll fresh from the oven. We've never held hands, not like this. It's nice … confusing, but nice.

I dart my gaze from our joined hands to his face and

back. He just gives me an amused smile and leans toward me. His closeness is even more pleasant than his hand holding. Maybe I've just put so much stress on this trip, and it's nice to have the comfort of a friend. This is the first time I've ever flown without my family. I know, pathetic, but … have you met my dad? I'm glad I'm here with Kemp and not on my own.

He nuzzles his nose in my hair, and an entirely different sensation spreads from the contact. I freeze, my eyes closing as I try to remember how to breathe. This. This is not comfort. That sparking along my hair and through my scalp is very much uncomfortable.

"The guy across the aisle keeps looking over here. I think he recognizes one of us." His words puff against my neck, and my breath shudders out of me.

Right. Our fake engagement. This might be harder than I originally thought.

It shouldn't surprise me that someone would recognize Kemp. Alley Oop has been advertising hard lately. Hopefully, Kemp is wrong, so we can just focus on getting our story straight.

He settles back into his chair and pulls up a game on his phone. His hand still holds mine lightly, and I love the feeling. When was the last time I held someone's hand without the anticipation of whether he was the one? Without nerves building at each touch? Maybe I *have* been putting too much weight into the whole first kiss thing.

I settle further into the seat and glance across the aisle. The man stares but quickly averts his eyes. I cock my head as I survey him. He looks vaguely familiar, so I sift through my memories from where I know him. He's in a business suit, and an expensive one by the cut and look of the material, yet he seems bridled somehow. Like the suit barely controls who he really is. Maybe it's the unruly way his hair sticks up in a messy do or the broad width of his shoulders that stretches the material tight. He'd make a magnificent portrait showing the juxtaposition of wild beauty restrained by culture.

His gaze darts across the aisle again, and I smile at him. His eyes widen before he ducks his head. The way his ears pink surprises me, and I've seen that before too. This memory is deep, like way in the depths of my thought ocean, but I feel it rising quickly.

He clears his throat, straightens in determination, and leans toward the aisle. "I'm sorry. I didn't mean to stare. It's just … you're Kemp Rees, right?"

Kemp puts his phone away and turns. "Yeah."

The man smiles, and the memory hits me.

Elementary school recess. I'm in first grade. Rory's in fifth. It's September 5th, a Wednesday, because we just ate pizza for lunch and the fire department is doing a talk right after recess. The sun shines warmly against my skin. She's sitting on the bench, reading a book like always. My chest heaves from playing chase and legs ache from running, so I plop down next to her.

"Whatcha reading?" I ask and peek at the words.

"Yeah, Meow, whatcha reading?" Dax Payton picks up the basketball that had raced across the court, slapping it between his hands. His smile is broad, slightly guilty, and completely menacing.

I shake my head to clear the memory and really look at the man across the aisle. Sure enough. Rory's elementary school nemesis sits there, handsome as get-out. Growing up sure looks good on him.

"Dax Payton." I don't ask. I know it's him.

He tilts his head at me, his eyes squinting. "Yeah."

"I'm Violet Wilde, Rory's cousin."

"Oh, yeah. It's been a while." His smile falters.

"Yep. At least since you used to terrorize my sweet cousin in fifth grade."

The blush on his neck darkens. "That was just stupid kid stuff. I meant nothing by it."

I should give him a hard time for it, but he's right. Most people grow out of their childhood idiocies, and those that don't leave a reputation behind them.

"What are you up to now? You look pretty snazzy for a boy with holes always in his jeans."

"I own the Body in Motion gyms."

"Oh, Rory goes there. She says it's really nice." I turn to Kemp. "Remember when she said that? She told us we should look into it. Surprised the daylights out of us that she was actually going somewhere to workout instead of just using the desk bike she has."

Kemp nods. "We made fun of her because she wouldn't go hiking with us, yet she'd go walking on the treadmill. But she likes it there, so whatever keeps her healthy."

Dax shifts in his seat and picks at his pant leg. "She really said that? I figured she only goes there because there're so few other places in Seward to go."

"Oh, no." I chuckle. "Whatever you're doing there, you're doing it right. She's fairly obsessed. She's usually only obsessed about one thing."

"Books."

All three of us say it at the same time, and I crack up laughing. The couple in front of Dax looks back with chiding expressions, like my behavior is not first class. I cringe and mouth, "Sorry."

"Well, I'm glad she's liking my gym." One side of Dax's mouth lifts before he stifles it with gruffness. "She's not complaining as much as she did when she first came in, so that's good."

I suppress my own smile at his interest in Rory and nudge my shoulder against Kemp's. "So, how do you know this guy?"

"Are you kidding me?" Dax's genuine grin returns as he looks at Kemp. "Not only have you won the Burton US Open the last four winters, snatched the gold at the Olympics, and dominated the X Games since you got on the scene, but you killed the Natural Selection Tour."

Now, Kemp's ears are red, and I can't contain my happiness for him. For the rest of the flight, getting our engagement story straight is put on hold as we talk about snowboarding. Surprisingly, I'm fine with it. I'd much rather have the memory of gushing about Kemp's awesomeness with Dax and completely embarrassing Kemp than one of Kemp and me getting our non-relationship lined out.

Chapter Twelve

-*KEMP*-

I trudge down the Grand Hyatt hotel hall after Violet, who is following a race official. The layover in Seattle turned into an all-night camp out in the terminal due to mechanical malfunctions with the plane. By the time they canceled the flight, it was too late (or early, I guess) to get a hotel and be back at the airport for our new flight at eight in the morning.

I can sleep just about anywhere. Yet, I'm on edge, worried even, and with every little noise that happened, I startled awake, my eyes instantly going to Violet to make sure she was safe. It didn't matter that I talked her into sleeping in a corner where the only way to her was by climbing over me. Yes, she had eye-rolled at that, but I didn't care. I will not break my promise to Will to keep her safe.

I'm also completely aware that I'm on edge because of Will and his "she's got issues" bit. I want to ask. I should ask, but I also want her to tell me herself. If I'm honest, I'm a little ticked she's keeping something from me. From Will's little trip to my place, it's something big.

Doesn't she trust me?

I trace my gaze along the slump in her shoulders. Some of her hair has fallen out of her bun, like blonde, purple, and turquoise streamers. I don't think she slept much, either. She hasn't brought up the topic of how we supposedly fell in love since we left Alaska. I know she thinks it will help, but sometimes the less you plan, the better things go. Our love and respect as friends will be enough to go on if people ask.

"Here's your room." The official turns and gives us a stern look. "Remember, you're not allowed to leave until you are called for the race start. If you open this door for any reason other than room service, security will alert the race officials, and you'll forfeit."

She points over her shoulder at a man camped out in a chair. Violet gives him a big wave. He presses his lips together and nods in acknowledgment.

"When will the race start?" Violet takes the key from the official's outstretched hand.

"Can't tell you. Just be ready, and make sure you read the rule book." With that, she stomps back down the hall.

"Well, then." I shake my head.

"She must be under a lot of stress with this." Violet, always looking at the good in people, stares after the woman with a tsk of compassion.

"Sure. That's it." I bump Violet's bag I insisted on carrying against her back. "I'm beat. Let's get in, order food, and crash."

"Right." She runs the key over the lock and steps into the room. "Oh."

It's a soft exclamation, but my head snaps up as I follow her into the room. One large bed is smack in the middle of the space. There's a desk by the window, next to a small lounge chair and ottoman. Besides the bathroom, that's it. My hands slick with sweat, and I drop her pack against the wall with a grunt.

"I didn't think about this." I swing my pack from my shoulders and plop it next to hers.

"It's kind of sad they just assume we sleep together since we're engaged." Violet's heavy sigh and delicate eyebrows gathering together make me want to fix this … to champion celibacy to anyone who would listen.

"I'll go down and ask for a new room." I turn to the door I'd let click shut behind me.

"No. Don't. She said we can't leave the room, remember?"

"I'll get the guard to call down. They can coordinate a move for us that will keep everything secret."

"Kemp, really. It's fine." She heads to the window and peeks out. "Though I wish they would've given us a view of the atrium instead of the street."

"I'll sleep on the floor."

"Kemp, chill, okay? That bed is bigger than any of the tents we've slept in together camping. I know you didn't sleep well last night. Neither of us did. If we're going to dominate the competition, we have to get a good night's sleep." She crosses back to me and grabs my biceps like she's giving me a pep talk. "It's not like we have to worry about our making out going too far or anything. That's the benefit of us being just friends."

She winks and whacks my arm. It's the truth. We have shared tents a lot smaller than the king-size bed. We also won't have the temptation to take things further than we should, since there will be no kissing to begin with.

So, why is there a dullness in my chest with that thought? I rub my hand over my heart and shake my head. It's probably just Will Wilde all up in my head.

"All right, but I'm telling them we need two beds from now on." I flop on top of the mattress face-first and moan at the soft comfort. "We should order room service before I'm too far gone to think about food."

Violet orders us food, then pulls the chair to the window. I turn my head from my face plant and watch as she surveys the world outside. Something catches her attention, and she cranes her neck to look down the street. The sun hits her hair just right, making it shine, and her full lips tip up in a surprised smile.

Man.

I swallow.

How have I never noticed how absolutely stunning she is?

I mean, I'm not blind or anything. She's always been pretty. It's just now … I don't know. She's different. Or I'm different. Which probably isn't good when you're getting ready to start the race of a lifetime.

Maybe I'm just tired.

My stomach growls.

And hungry.

Yeah, that's my problem. Lack of sleep and food has my brain loopy.

"Did I ever tell you about the last time I came to D.C.?" Violet asks, though she's now looking down the street the opposite way.

"No."

"It was a week-long trip in high school. We came

to watch the legislature proceedings and visit our representatives." She finally glances over at me, and my heart skips at how the sun highlights her cheek. "Spent an obscene amount of time walking to just about every museum possible, which will come in handy. It's an advantage that the start of the race is here."

I push up onto my elbows. "Why's that?"

She bites the corner of her bottom lip and averts her eyes to the painting over the bed. "I have a pretty good memory."

"What, like photographic?"

Violet's face scrunches in indecision.

"No. Well—"

A knock raps on the door, and the crease in her forehead relaxes into relief. Why won't she tell me? I sit up as a ball of steel settles in my stomach. She really doesn't trust me, does she?

"Thank goodness. I'm starving." Violet crosses to the desk. "Let's set up dinner here. I'll read through the rules as we eat so we can go to sleep. I don't think I can keep my eyes open much longer."

I groan as I get up from the bed. It's a good thing the food arrived fast. I can't stay awake much longer, either, especially with how comfortable the bed is. I plop into the chair Violet pulled up to the desk and take the lid off the food.

"Mmm. This is amazing." Violet talks around a mouthful of burger, making me chuckle.

My smile fades as I look at the tired circles under her eyes. That dullness in my chest shifts to an ache that makes it hard to breathe. Why is she keeping something from me? She's my best friend, the only person I've ever fully had faith in. It hurts to think she doesn't trust me in the same way.

"You know …" I clear my throat as I dredge a fry through the dipping sauce. "You know I love you, right? That you can tell me anything, and it won't change our friendship. If at any point in this race you want to call it quits, just say the word and we're done. I don't want to make you uncomfortable or anything."

She sets down her burger, her eyes darting from one of mine to the other like she's searching for the real reason I just said that. Her smile is soft, tender, making that ache in my chest throb with the thuggish beat of my heart. She puts her hand on my arm and squeezes.

"Rees, you're my best friend. I know pretending to be engaged and everything that comes with that is awkward." She tips her chin to the bed looming at my side. "But we have a chance to do something amazing here, and I trust you one hundred percent. Not only to keep me as physically safe as you can, but to protect me in all the other ways that matter. Just like I'll always protect you too."

She leans over and gives me a peck on the cheek before hugging me and returning to her meal. It's not exactly what I wanted to hear, but her words ease the ache, anyway. Whatever it is her dad is worried about, she'll tell me if and when she's ready. Until then, I'll just be on guard to help her "process."

Chapter Thirteen

-Violet-

I scan the other teams as we gather around the race's host, Jill Probert. There's a team of basketball players, a couple from another reality TV show, the brother-sister duo that created the Marshpillow for wilderness camping and made it go viral on TikTok, and the tennis team that won the Olympics last year. The other teams I don't recognize, though I think one of them has something to do with NASCAR racing. A memory is swimming beneath my feet about him, but I need to push it down and focus on the now. Who the other teams are doesn't matter, at least not at this moment.

"Teams, welcome to the Race Across the Americas!" Jill lifts her hands out to her side, her face open with excitement.

I'm glad she's hosting the race. I've always enjoyed her extreme travel show on the Nature Channel. Having her here seems like I have another friend cheering me on, which is utter ridiculousness since we've never actually met.

Who we do have silently cheering us on is Bo Kang. Peeking back at our shadow for the race, I give a big thumbs up for the camera. I can't believe Ivy let Bo be our cameraman. I thought for sure my weird request would've been shot down, especially if some considered it an advantage. Not that Bo would help us win.

"Are you ready to go on the most amazing race you've ever been on?" Jill looked at everyone, clasping her hands in front of her.

The teams' cheers hit me with a pop of adrenaline and boost my already pumped body. I place my fingers in my mouth and let off an ear-splitting whistle. Kemp smiles at me and rubs his ear closest to me. I never fail to impress him with that whistle.

"This race will be like none ever held before. There will be no eliminations, so no matter where you are in the lineup, there's always a chance you'll still win. There are also no time limits, so no matter how long you take to finish a challenge, you'll still be required to complete it to move onto the next one." She pauses and scans all of us. "You'll be tested both physically and mentally, probably more than you've ever been your entire life. Think you can handle it?"

From the yells that go up around the circle, we are ready for it. The teams I know are as up for extreme adventures as Kemp and I are. The fierce competition bounces me from foot to foot in anticipation.

"All right. It sounds like I've been talking long enough. Are you ready to find your way through the Americas?" Jill holds her hands high like those ladies that start drag races. When the tension has built like a bubble about to burst, she drops her arms and yells, "Go!"

Kemp and I race away from the other teams and stop to rip open the clue. I read along as he reads out loud.

Waves of soldiers who answered the call.
Immortalized forever, etched in the wall.

"It has to be on the National Mall." Kemp looks at me. "That's where all the war monuments are, right?"

"Yeah." The words whirl in my head, memories swirling up from my visit here in high school.

"Run or cab?" He stuffs the clue into the front pocket of his pack and swings it onto his shoulders.

While we waited in the hotel, I had studied the map in the information folder in the desk drawer. From the hotel, the National Mall is only two miles away. The park they'd walked us to a few blocks west from the Hyatt would be the same, maybe closer. We both can run fast, even with our heavy packs on our backs.

"Run." I take off down the street, pulling up the map in my brain as we cross K Street NW to head down 14th Street NW.

It might be a mistake to go by foot. Probably, since most of the other teams are hollering for taxis. But the traffic crawls right now, so hopefully I haven't made a miscalculation.

"Waves of soldiers etched in the wall. It doesn't make much sense." Kemp keeps pace beside me, working out the clue now that the other teams aren't close. "Waves of soldiers make me think of Normandy and that Tom Hanks movie when they crash onto the beach. Yet, the wall is the Vietnam War."

We stop to wait at a light. I'm shuffling through the playbacks of my memories as fast as I can, like I'm scanning through the selections on Netflix. The answer is there. I know it is. I just have to focus on the right memory. It's so close, but it's taking its time coming from the depths.

"Wilde, you okay?" Kemp's hand on my elbow startles me.

I jerk and glance around at the traffic. "Yeah."

"You just kind of zoned out for a minute there." Kemp's eyes scrunch in concern.

"I was thinking, trying to remember something." The light changes, and I take off across the street.

"I guess you could say the Vietnam wall is in a wave the way it curves. Maybe." Kemp's huffing as he talks. "Wait. The World War II memorial has that fountain, and I'm pretty sure there is a representation of the soldiers who fought."

"There're just over 4,000 gold stars, each representing a hundred Americans who died in the war. 405,399 lives lost in that war." I spit out the facts like a tour guide.

"How in the world did you remember that?" Kemp puts his hands on his head as we wait at another light.

"I just do."

I can't answer him fully now, not when I'm so close. I slide the memories before me, going through each of the monuments and museums I visited when here in high school. My eyes widen as a face in stainless steel gazes at me. His weary stare and gun poised at the ready haunts me.

Tears blur my vision, and I blink to clear them. Of course. I should've thought of the Korean War Veterans Memorial right away. I'm going to have to focus, not let the stress of the race impede my superpower.

"I know where we need to go." I take off across the street, not waiting for everyone to stop.

Kemp snags my arm and yanks me out of the way of a car running a red light. The driver honks at us, but we keep going.

"Let's not get run over on the first leg, okay?" Kemp holds up his hand to another car honking.

The noise and constant blaring of horns is a memory I purposely pushed deep. It's startling and makes my head hurt. Living in Alaska all my life did nothing to prepare my ears for the assault.

"Where are we going?" Kemp asks.

I look behind us to make sure no other teams are near. The closest team is two blocks away. Did the others hop in cabs?

"Korean War Veterans Memorial."

"I've never heard of that one."

"Exactly. It's kind of off to the side among the trees. We almost missed it when we were here for school." I suck in a big breath as my chest burns. Okay, maybe running two miles with twenty-five pound packs wasn't the best idea. "It's my favorite memorial by far. So incredibly poignant. There's a wall with faces of servicemen and women etched upon it in a series of waves. When you look at it from afar, it looks like the mountain ranges in Korea. Seriously. It's just like … ugh." I inhale air like I'm starving. "So memorable."

"Okay. Korean Wall. Here we come." Kemp pats my pack. "Good job."

"It's on the south side of the Lincoln Memorial Reflecting Pool." I picture the map. "We'll have to be careful passing the World War II Memorial if anyone is there."

Fifteen minutes later, we cross Constitution Avenue. The Washington Monument is on our left as we veer off the sidewalk along 12th for a path through the trees. If someone drives by, I hope the trees block us from them. Our feet slap loud against the pavement, and people milling about stop and watch us race past.

When the World War II Memorial comes into view, I slow down and take the sidewalk that will skirt around the outside of the monument along the reflecting pool. Stopping at the tree line, I point across the gap where we'll likely be seen if others are at the memorial.

"Do we just nonchalantly walk across and hope we blend in with the crowd, or do we make a break for it?" I point to the trees lining the south side of the long rectangular pool. "The Korean War memorial is tucked back in those trees, so once we get past this open space, we should be hidden from both the street and the other memorials."

Kemp scans the area, ducking to peer into the gaps in the World War II Memorial. We're both breathing hard, and sweat saturates my back and runs down my hairline. Yuck. I wipe my forehead and cheek with the back of my hand. It's a good thing I'm not too big on my looks and didn't put any makeup on this morning, besides waterproof mascara, otherwise I'd be stressing my face was melting into a freaky clown. I'll take the cool temps of Alaska any day over this sticky, thick air.

"Let's stroll," Kemp says with a nod.

He takes my hand and pulls me into a casual walk

down the sidewalk, like it was an everyday occurrence to have your personal cameraman following you. It's strange, really, having people staring and whispering to their companions, but no one actually talking to you. The few I smile at either quickly avert their eyes like it embarrasses them to be caught staring or giggle like I'm someone famous or something. Maybe I'll get used to it the further the race goes.

As we pass the World War II Memorial, two teams scramble out of cabs on the opposite side. I pull Kemp faster to get us behind a pillar. I'm pretty sure they didn't see us, but I don't want to take any chances.

"Two teams just arrived." I look over my shoulder and find the teams running up to the monument.

Kemp drags me into a tour group just leaving the monument.

"Smart." I smile up at him.

"Hopefully." He shrugs, scanning beyond the group, then behind. "Maybe if someone sees the camera, they'll think it's for the tour and not us."

As the guide tells us about the depth of the reflecting pool and other information most will forget in five minutes, we edge our way to the south side of the group. At the first small sidewalk shooting through the trees, we break off from the protection of the crowd and book it through the trees. We cut across the lawn and sprint the rest of the way to the Korean War Memorial.

"Keep your eyes open. We don't want to miss the clue." Kemp slows to a walk as we approach the monument.

What kind of saying is that? Of course, I'm going to keep my eyes open. I roll them, then realize I'm not paying attention to my surroundings. That's when I see the first statue, and the depth of sacrifice hits me again. I grab Kemp's hand and thread my fingers through his.

He looks at me, then darts his gaze around. "What? What's wrong?"

"Look, Kemp. Take a moment, and let this memory settle."

I let my eyes roam over the statues posed like they're walking through a rice field, then past them to the black granite wall reflecting the statues, doubling the troop to thirty-eight quiet men, putting their lives on the line for a people they didn't know. The faces etched into the wall are too far to see much detail, but my memories of them float up to layer upon what's before me. A tear spills from my lashes, but I don't wipe it away.

"'Freedom is not free.' That's what the wall beyond the Pool of Remembrance says." I take a deep breath and squeeze Kemp's hand. His anxiety to go buzzes off of him, so him not rushing me swells more tears to tangle in my lashes. Good thing I wore the waterproof mascara. "Memories are hard sometimes. They like to push their way to the surface and overwhelm, but it's good that we don't forget this and all the people who fight and die for our freedom."

Kemp squeezes my hand back. "Thanks for making me slow down. I wouldn't have really seen this if I hadn't."

I gaze up at him. "Let's make sure we do that, that we actually be in these moments and places instead of just race through them. I'd rather lose and have an ocean full of memories with you, than win and have just a blur."

His smile is tender, and his eyes hold something I've never seen in them before. He reaches with the hand not held in mine and tucks a loose strand of hair behind my ear. His fingers leave a trail of tingling skin where he touches, and my breath catches in my throat for an entirely different reason.

"I like that thought." He tips his head toward the rest of the monument. "Ready?"

I nod, my voice not working at the moment. Bo comes up beside me, and the camera startles me back to reality. I swallow, feeling silly for putting more into Kemp's touch than there was. Of course, that was the perfect time to give a little engagement show for the masses. I blink back the sting of disappointment, not understanding why it's there to begin with.

"Vi, look."

Kemp points to the pool and pulls me toward it. Past the trees circling the pool hangs a pouch from another tree about a hundred yards beyond the memorial. We probably wouldn't have ever seen it if we hadn't taken the moment to pause.

"See. Sometimes slowing down is the best thing to do," I say as we rush past the pool and across the grass.

"Sometimes." Kemp grabs my pack and helps me out of it. "But not now. Scamper up there, little squirrel."

He laces his fingers into a brace and bends down. His boost up is more of a toss, and I scramble to hold on to the branch before I crash down. I wrap my leg around the branch when the tree gets frisky, shoving its limb up my shirt and almost pulling it off. With one hand, I'm clinging to the branch with a death grip. With the other, I'm trying to yank the leaves and twigs jammed up my shirt so I can pull the fabric back over my belly.

"Babe, I know you're hot and not used to this humidity, but you've got to keep your shirt on. This is a family show." Kemp laughs and winks at the camera.

The problem is he's not far from the truth. I'm sweating everywhere. Really, I've never sweated behind my knees before. It's disgusting.

"Very funny." I grunt, as I finally stop the tree from feeling me up and adjust my grip on the limb. I bend my head down so I'm looking at him upside-down, my loose hair reaching toward the ground. "Next time you boost me up, tone down the muscles, Hulk."

"You can't tone these bad boys down, Wilde. Not possible." He flexes his bicep and kisses it.

I roll my eyes and monkey my way down the branch. The bark is smooth and slippery under my sweaty hands. When I get close, I stretch my hand toward the pouch. Just as I'm pulling the envelope out of the pouch, my other hand slips. The sudden shift in weight and sweaty skin on my legs slides my hold on the branch loose. My stomach jettisons into my throat, capturing my scream as the ground rushes toward my face.

Kemp catches me with a grunt, and we both crash to the ground. My pulse pounds in my ears, drowning out all other sounds. I lay my cheek on Kemp's chest. His heart thumps fast against my face. He was just as scared as I was.

"You okay?" He pushes the hair off of my eyes.

"Yeah. Thanks for breaking my fall." I put my chin on his chest and smile up at him.

"I will always catch you, Violet." He rubs his fingers across my cheek, and my heart that had just gotten back to normal-beats per minute jumps back into overdrive. "Always."

"Come on. We can't be lying around." I push off of him, making him groan.

As he gets to his feet, he snags the envelope from the grass. He rips it open and reads aloud.

Your first leg may be easy, but your next will not be so breezy.

"That was easy?" I grumble.

Trek to the desert adorned by arches where Indiana Jones's father charges.

"Moab." Kemp shoves the clue in the envelope.

"What?" I can't believe he got Moab from that brief line.

"We're going to Moab. *Indiana Jones and the Last Crusade* was filmed there." He picks me up and spins me in a circle. "You're amazing. I can't believe you remembered this monument was here."

He sets me down, sliding his fingers back through mine. "Come on. Let's get out of here before anyone else shows up."

As we take off to find a cab, I will my heart to stop palpitating. It was the two-mile sprint that has it pounding out of my chest. Has to be. Because there is no way I can let it beat erratically for Kemp. Not when that puts our friendship in danger.

Chapter Fourteen

-KEMP-

I scan the red rock desert of eastern Utah as the sun crests the mountains to the east. The stark landscape dotted with cactus and sagebrush against the towers of muted red amaze me like it always does. There's something about the beauty of this area that infuses into my soul and soothes me.

It's why I had spent those two months here my first summer after I left home. I came with some guys I'd met on the slope for a weekend and left eight weeks later when training started. Hopefully, my time here will give us an advantage over the other teams.

By the time we departed Virginia, two other teams had arrived. The lead I had hoped we'd have for the first leg disappeared. Did Violet care? Nope. She walked right up to them and made friends.

Fortunately, they flew into Salt Lake City, while I picked landing in Grand Junction, Colorado. My hope that the shorter drive would get us to Moab first paid off. Out of the teams that got in yesterday, we were the first to arrive, which means we get a thirty-minute head start. While I'd like it to be a bigger gap, the competition will keep us on our toes.

I turn off the highway and head down a dirt road into the desert. There are some great hiking and climbing areas on this road. Maybe our luck will keep shining on us and this leg will be something I've done before. Not that I believe in luck.

"You used to live here?" There's something in Violet's voice that pulls my eyes to her in the rearview mirror.

Actually, it's been hard to keep my eyes off of her. Ever since D.C. and that stupid hotel room, my mind keeps focusing on things it shouldn't. Like how soft her hair is or how the twinkle in her eyes makes me want to keep it there forever. Would they ever sparkle in awe at me?

Who am I kidding? My brain created problems well before the hotel. When I slid my hand into hers on the plane after catching Dax looking at her, it was totally a chest thumping, Neanderthal-claiming move. I may have justified it as keeping up the fake engagement, but having her small fingers threaded through mine had nothing to do with pretend relationships. Not really.

Looking at her now, staring out the window, longing practically radiating off her, I can't believe I never considered that maybe I'd already found my soulmate. Granted, I hadn't been too serious about looking. Yet, you'd think that I would've noticed, right? She tears her eyes from the passing landscape and cocks her eyebrow up at me in the mirror.

"I didn't really live here." I clear my throat when my

voice comes out all weird and garbled. "Just spent a few months one summer."

"That must have been amazing." She turns back to the mountains and sagebrush with a sigh. "I wish I had brought more colors with me."

She'd spent the flights to Grand Junction drawing in a spiral bound art book she'd brought. I've always been impressed with the realism she somehow creates in her chaotic array of colors but watching her work with nothing but a package of colored pencils was something else. I'm still trying to figure out how she can remember all the finite details of the statues at the Korean War Veterans Memorial like she did. It doesn't seem possible, even with a photographic memory.

"I'll bring you back here. Show you all that Moab and the surrounding area has to offer." The rental car hits a rut, and I jerk my gaze back out the windshield.

"Really?" The hopefulness of her voice pulls my gaze right back to her.

"Yeah." I swallow and force my eyes to look away and act normal. I can't show her the way my thoughts are creating chaos in my brain. Not when I promised nothing would change between us. "The camping and hiking here are amazing. We can do mountain biking, climbing, whitewater rafting, lots of stuff. Just when you think you've seen it all, you find another little trail to follow that leads to a new treasure."

"I'd like that." Her laugh flits through the air, and I inhale a breath to catch the joy in my lungs. "If we win, maybe we can take the rest of the summer off, rent a RV, and take our time trekking across America."

"I'm game."

I'm such a glutton for punishment. If I'm having a

hard time keeping our friendship front and center now, how am I going to do it after we finish racing across the world, not able to be more than ten feet from each other? I thought that rule was silly when Violet read it. Now, it seems more like torture.

"Oh, look." Violet sits up and points. "We must be here."

I pull into the parking area marked with the blue and red flags of the race. Anticipation hums just under my skin. I hope the challenge is physical. The need to burn off the jitters is almost as bad as when I was in elementary school and had to stay inside during recess.

Violet smiles back at me as she opens the clue box. Those jitters humming switch to a full out buzz. Rolling my shoulders doesn't dissipate it. She rips open the clue and reads.

Two choices you have:
1. Dive into history.
2. Soar over geography.

She shakes her head and rubs her hand over her forehead. "I know nothing about the history of the area." She closes her eyelids, and her eyes move behind her lids like she's searching. "Like nothing. It's empty."

Why is she so upset by not knowing? Unless you grew up in an area, the most any of us get for history is maybe a week or two during social studies in school. Even then, there probably wasn't much detail. I can't honestly say I remember learning anything about Moab before I stayed here.

"It's okay."

I grab her hand and pull her down the trail. Sure, I

could have just walked and she would have followed, but I needed to feel the zing of her skin against mine like some junkie needing a hit. Even if it's just for a moment.

"Besides, I say we check out the soaring bit. Hang gliding and base jumping would be more thrilling than learning a bunch of history." When the buzz running up my arm threatens to short-circuit my brain, I squeeze her hand and let go. "I think I need something exciting right now."

We hike for about thirty minutes through the scorching heat of the Utah desert. This is one thing I don't miss about being here. Alaska summers are much more pleasant. Sure, sometimes the clouds and cool temps get to me, but it never stifles like this. At least we aren't somewhere humid like D.C.

"No." Violet gasps ahead of me.

She's been gushing the entire hike about one thing or another. A scurrying lizard here. The blooming cactus there. Thankfully, her pace kept steady. This fearful exclamation has the hair on the back of my neck rising. I rush to her side just in time to see a mountain biker zoom down a steep incline and rocket over empty space.

"Oh, yeah!" I yell.

"Rees, no." Violet barely whispers her disagreement.

I bump her shoulder as I pass, my grin so wide my cheeks hurt. This is exactly the type of challenge I need to get my focus off Violet and back on the race. If I can get the weight of keeping things friendly while making the world think we are engaged off my shoulders, even for a handful of seconds, I'll take it.

Chapter Fifteen

-*Violet*-

I can't help the shake of my head as the mountain biker, Chaz, goes over what the challenge is. This is beyond crazy. One wrong move and Kemp is in the hospital or worse.

"Rees, really. We can go to the other station and learn whatever it is we need to." I grab his arm and hug it to my body as my stomach clenches. "Please, you getting hurt isn't worth it."

"It'll be fine." He wraps his arm I'm strangling around my back and gazes into my eyes. "I've got this. Remember, I spent two months riding trails around here."

"So, you've done this before?" My belly relaxes slightly. Why worry if he's done this?

"Not exactly." Kemp hedges with the best of them.

"How exactly?"

I place my hand on his chest. If I have to, I'll fist his shirt in my fingers and drag him to the other station. He probably won't make a scene with the way he avoids drama.

His heart pounds rapidly against my palm. Energy and excitement vibrate off him, and it's hard to keep a level head. I'm the crazy Wilde woman, the one who will skim down a rope out of a helicopter and free climb ice walls without a second thought. So why does it feel like my heart is pounding right out of my chest?

"I've jumped before, just not this steep." He wraps his fingers around mine, kisses my knuckles, sending a zing of electricity as if I grabbed an electric eel, then pulls me toward the cliff like he didn't just leave my head spinning with his affection. "It's all about momentum. All I have to do is keep the bike straight. The motion of the bike does the rest."

"Do you want to see it again?" Chaz asks.

I nod, mainly because I don't want my voice to crack and look like a scaredy cat on television. Maybe if I watch closely, I can see what Kemp means.

Chaz motions to the experts chatting at the start of the challenge. A woman hops on her bike and pedals toward the cliff edge. The bike and rider shoot off the edge and soar to the bottom of the hill. When they land, the bike whooshes up the other side of the canyon. The rider pedals at the end to make another smaller jump over about ten feet of rugged rocks onto a skinny trail on the opposite cliff.

Kemp's right about momentum. If anyone can do it, he can. Doesn't mean I like the thought of him giving this physics lesson a try.

"Okay." I lean my forehead on his shoulder and huff. "Just … don't break your neck or face or anything important. A leg or arm, even a rib, is fine. But not the head."

His laugh hums against my cheek as he wraps his arms around me in a hug. "What? You worried I'll mess up my handsome mug?"

"No. I'm worried you'll scramble your brains, and I'll spend my life spoon-feeding you watery oatmeal."

He stills, his breath catching in his chest. Did I say something wrong and blow our cover? I think through what I just said but can't figure out what would have him freeze. He leans his head against mine, his breath shuddering out into my hair.

"Okay … no scrambling brains." He rubs my back in comfort, and I take a fortifying breath.

"Give him a kiss for good luck and zip on across the way to wait for him." Chaz claps Kemp on the shoulder and heads to the group of bikers.

I pull back and look up at Kemp. He tilts his head and shrugs, his mouth hitched slightly up on one side in apology. I'm not sure I can do this.

What about my one kiss rule?

If I kiss him and it's just like the others, won't that make our friendship awkward? If there is a sizzle or spark, won't that be worse? There's never been more than friendship between Kemp and me, even if he's doing a good job pretending there is. I can't confuse the excitement of the race for stirrings or whatever for Kemp. I don't want to fight the drowning memory of heartbreak, especially not with him. When this race is over, he'll expect to somehow amicably break the engagement off.

How exactly will we do that without exposing that our relationship was fake to begin with? We really should have thought about that more. I can't lose my friendship with Kemp over this.

He pats my back softly, letting me know it's okay to just let this kiss go. But it's not okay, not if we want to keep the charade up. I'll just kiss him on the cheek and give him a big hug. That should be enough.

Lifting onto my toes, I watch his face for clues. As he stares down at me, his eyes soften and the muscles in his shoulders relax. His fingers flex in the back of my shirt, making my stomach flip.

I veer toward his mouth. The soft touch of my lips to his shouldn't make my breath catch in my throat, but it does. If I was smart, I would have stuck with the plan and kissed his cheek. Apparently, I should be worried about my brain, not his.

His hand flattens on my back with his exhale, like he wants to keep me close. The pressure of his palm spanning my back sends warmth through my body, like all my cells finally aligned and are buzzing with excitement.

I keep my eyes closed through another inhale, wanting to process this moment. To cherish it. I finally look at Kemp, and he doesn't break eye contact. He takes a large, deep breath like he's savoring the moment, then leans his forehead to mine.

"I'll see you on the other side."

I've never heard his low and gravelly tone before. My chest squeezes like I'm wrapped in a ratchet strap. When he steps away, the invisible strap tightens like someone is pumping the handle. I can't breathe.

Someone touches my shoulder, but I barely feel it. "This way, miss."

I follow the lady to a zip line stretched between the two mountains, and she hooks me up. Flying over the beautiful red desert should thrill me. Yet, my mind keeps cycling through that small, lovely kiss, replaying every millisecond in fast motion, making me lightheaded.

The rush of wind against my face as the ground disappears beneath my feet jolts me to the present in time to stop myself from crashing into the attendants on the other side of the canyon. Wasn't it just yesterday that I told Kemp to experience each moment we're on this race? I need to snap out of it, but my body trembles. The attendant disconnects me from the harness, and I wipe a shaky hand across my lips as I look over the gap at Kemp, preparing for the jump.

Maybe I'm just afraid of him making it across in one piece.

My stupid brain flashes to the look in Kemp's eyes before I kissed him and the pull of my shirt around my ribs as he fisted it in his hand. I shudder out a painful breath as my heart thuds against my ribs so hard I'm positive the viewers can see it on the screen.

Kemp tests the spring to the bike and raises his hand, signaling he's ready. Sweat pools in my pits even though I used extra-strength antiperspirant. The only problem is I'm not sure if I'm more afraid of Kemp taking the jump or of where that kiss leaves our friendship.

The two teams that had taken the plane to Salt Lake run up the trail just as Kemp settles on the bike, and the people gathered back up to give him space. He rocks forward and back on the seat once … twice, and I cover my mouth with my fingers to keep from screaming for him to stop. Then, he pedals across the flat ridge at full speed.

When he hits the edge and rockets into the air, my

entire body suspends in time like I'm the one free falling to the desert floor. His form is perfect as the bike lands and rushes up the opposite side of the canyon toward me. He wobbles right before he hits the jump, and the bike takes to the air at a sideways angle. The crowd "oh's" in collected concern.

I can't look away, but I don't want this memory.

His back tire catches the very edge of the trail. Kemp throws his weight over the handlebars and pedals. The bike slips but, at the last moment, digs into the dirt and takes him to the waiting crowd.

My vision blurs as relief collects in my eyes. Kemp rips off his helmet and holds it up in triumph. I laugh choppily, then exhale all the tension bottling up in me. He leaves the bike and races to me, picking me up in a bear hug and swinging me around.

"See. Nothing to it." He puts me down, his smile beaming with pride and happiness.

I can't make things awkward for us, so I shrug. "Eh. No big deal."

"Right?" He drapes his arm across my shoulders and turns us to look across the gap. "That was a rush. I haven't felt like that since snowboarding that mountain behind Valdez. Remember that?"

I do. Kemp and I have lots of memories floating in my ocean, waiting to be pulled up to the surface. Why hadn't I ever realized before how often I grab for them?

"Yeah, but I think I'll leave this ride for just you."

He cups his hands around his mouth, and I miss the weight of his arm on me.

"You jumping?" He hollers across to the other teams.

"We're not crazy!" One of the tall basketball players,

Tyrone, yells back, swatting his hands at Kemp like he was nuts before heading farther along the ridge to the other station.

"Looks like we have another lead." Kemp smiles down at me and pulls me to the person holding the next clue.

My gaze lingers on the tilt of his lips before I force my attention to where it should be, which is getting to the next leg before the other teams. We might be ahead in the race, but my thoughts still lag on that kiss. If I can't shake the fear and doubt loose, then we lose … in more ways than one.

Chapter Sixteen

My gaze darts to Violet sleeping in the back seat of the rental, for the millionth time since we left Moab to drive to Las Vegas. Finally, the worry lines on her forehead have relaxed. They hadn't left her face since she'd kissed me, and I'm not sure if it's the peck or the lack of clue to the next challenge that has her worried.

Part of me wants to ask her about that kiss. Sure, it was just a quick touch, but it roared to life all my feelings for her that had simmered under the surface without me knowing. Yes, there's attraction and a desire to protect, but, more than that, there's a love I never expected. And it's not a friendly sort of love, though that's a big reason for why it's so strong.

Another part of me is terrified she'll stick to her silly one-kiss rule. Sorry, I know it's not silly. She has her reasons, and if she ever tells me why, I'm sure I'll find them valid.

I guess I'm worried she won't break that rule. And I'm so desperate for her to take a second chance on me

116

that nervous energy rattles my body. My leg hasn't stopped bouncing since I slid into the car. If I can just get her to kiss me again, maybe we can make a habit of it. If we make a habit of it, maybe, just maybe, I can convince her to make this fake relationship real.

We crest a hill, and Vegas's lights fill the horizon. It's been a long, exhausting day, and I'm hoping this challenge will include a mandatory pit stop. Or at least a long flight when it's done.

"Vi, we're getting close." I reach my hand through the gap in the front seats and jostle her knee.

Did I need to?

Nope.

Did I want the excuse to be close, even for just a second?

Absolutely.

I know. I'm pathetic. Honestly, I don't even care. Violet's worth being pathetic for.

Bo snorts a snore next to me in the passenger seat and jerks awake. It's a good thing he could just mount one of his cameras on the dash and another in the backseat for filming, otherwise he might be fired. Not that there was anything worth broadcasting the last six hours since we left Moab.

"Oh, wow." Violet gasps from the back and leans over the console. "It's so beautiful."

The expanse of lights spreading through the desert valley never fails to impress. To go from desolate interstate to so much brightness makes my palms sweat. I haven't decided if it's in excitement or anxiety. After moving to Alaska, cities like Vegas make me itch.

"Yeah. It's okay." I turn and look at her profile. "You ready for jostling crowds?"

"Yes." She cringes. "No. It's a little terrifying, which is dumb because I'm a grown woman and love people."

"It's different from Alaska, even when we get busy in the summer." I gaze back out the window. "Don't worry. I'm sure we'll have a blast."

Thirty minutes later, we pull into the parking lot for Treasure Island. I help Violet into her pack, then we rush through the crowd to the battling ships display on the Strip. A pirate captain greets us with a "Huzzah!" and hands us the next clue. I pull Violet to the wood fence surrounding the water for the pirate show as she reads the clue out loud.

What happens in Vegas, stays in Vegas.
Or does it?
Immerse yourself in something quintessentially Vegas.
Then make your way to the Bay.
Remember, keep your wits along the Strip.
It's essential for a profitable stay.

"Okay, what the heck does all that mean?" I scratch my head as Violet slides another paper from the envelope.

"Well, I think the checkpoint is at the Mandalay Bay. Isn't that a hotel here?" she asks and continues when I nod. "There are some suggestions on what are Vegas events. Things like: learn the art of hypnotization, become a pirate, win a fortune, train to float the canal. That kind of stuff ... well, and other stuff I'm not willing to do." Her blush is cute as it crawls up her cheeks. "Whatever we do has to be approved, and this is also a mandatory, eight-hour pit stop."

"Thank goodness. I'm beat." I grab the sheet of

suggestions from her hand. "We should get the challenge done first. That way, we can figure out how to get to the next leg as quickly as possible after the break. What do you think?"

"Yeah. Sounds good," she answers, but I don't really think she heard me.

She has this far-off look on her face, like she's not really here. A crowd has gathered, and several of them have their phones out, videoing us. (Like having one constant cameraman trailing us isn't enough.) A group of older women point behind us. I turn to see if another team has arrived, only to find Violet and me live on a Jumbotron on the side of the hotel.

She's now chewing on her bottom lip, and her eyebrows scrunch. I turn back to Violet. Are her processing issues Will warned me about going to cause her harm or embarrassment here? I wish Will had told me more. Or, better yet, that she had told me.

"Vi? You okay?" I rub my hand down her arm and squeeze her hand.

"I know what we should do." She swallows and finally looks at me.

"Okay. What floats your fancy?" I glance at the list of suggestions again.

One woman from the group pressing in on us shouts, "What are you going to do?"

"We should get married." Violet rushes the words out.

I shake my head to clear the noise from the crowd.

"I'm sorry, what?" I lean closer because there is no way Violet said what I think she said.

"Let's get married." Her yell above the din leaves no confusion this time.

The group of women clap and bounce up and down in celebration like it's one of them getting hitched. Violet smiles at them before turning back to me. I shake my head again, though this time in disbelief.

"Vi, there are other things we can do. We don't have to get married." Realizing that my comment might expose our fake engagement, I rush on. "I know you want your family at the wedding."

"Kemp, it's perfect. I don't think any of the other teams can do this." She grabs my hand, and I want to agree so badly my jaw hurts from clenching my teeth together. "I had a friend from high school get married here, and she said it literally took less than an hour from getting the license to saying, 'I do.'" When I rub the back of my neck with my free hand, she squeezes my hand even harder. "Come on. Marry me."

I gaze down at her. Turquoise, purple, and blonde strands stick wildly from the bun she threw her hair in while we drove into town. Her light blue eyes hold determination and fire, and I want nothing more than to say yes.

But where would that leave us after the race?

If we get married, I'm not letting her go. She's the one who challenges me to be better, try harder, even though she's always accepted me for who I am. When I'm with her, I'm more myself than anywhere else.

When I'm with her … I'm home.

I was an idiot for taking so long to realize it. Maybe because she's the best friend I've ever had. Maybe I didn't want to see how much she meant to me, how much I loved her, because I didn't want to mess up the one relationship that put me back together after my messed-up childhood. It doesn't matter the reason because I'm not blind to her importance now.

I want the days the race will provide to convince her to marry me for real.

"It'll be fine, Kemp." She brings my hand up under her chin and wraps the other hand around it. "We'll figure out details later."

The crowd chants for me to say yes. I barely hear them over the roar of my pulse in my ears. Violet smiles with her teeth together and bats her eyes in an exaggerated plea. I never want her to beg for anything.

"I'd love to have you as my wife, Violet." I lift our hands to my lips and kiss her knuckles. "If that's what you want, I'll marry you."

For a split second, her pleading look melts into confusion, which she quickly masks when cheers erupt from the crowd. We get jostled with congratulations. I want to tuck Violet under my arm and escape, but the group of women pull Violet into a hug and rattle on about what needs done.

I'm so over my head right now with nerves and worry. I wanted to get Violet to walk down the aisle to me without an escape clause attached. But if the years shredding it down the most treacherous slopes the world offers have taught me anything, I'm good at changing mid-course. I'll just have to use the rest of the race to convince Violet that the only details we need to figure out is whose place we're moving into when we get home.

Chapter Seventeen

I smooth my hand down the satin dress my new friends, Maggie and Sheila, rented at the Downtown Tux & Gown Rentals. I had hastily put it on in the dressing room in Vegas Weddings where Donna and Bev scheduled my elopement to Kemp while we obtained our marriage license across the street for the ceremony.

The ceremony happening any minute.

My stomach flips and head swims. I swallow down the nerves and look at the women helping with the finishing touches.

Did they agree to help for their fifteen-seconds of fame or because they truly are excited? I'm going to go with the latter to help ease my nerves and conscience over this rash decision, especially since they remind me of my grandma and her group of friends that are always up to something. I'm thankful they'll be a part of this memory. Their kindheartedness and enthusiasm are just what I need to keep me from bolting out the back door.

"See, Sheila, I told you this dress would be gorgeous

on her." Maggie crosses her arms and raises an eyebrow at Sheila.

"You were right. I'll never underestimate your fashion sense again." Sheila rolls her eyes as she pulls a curl over my shoulder. "I'll never hear the end of it, dearie. For the rest of our days, she'll drone on and on about how she single-handedly got you married."

"Why, I never—" Maggie sputters, her mouth dropping wide in disbelief.

"Now, Sheila. She won't brag for the rest of our lives." Donna bumps Sheila's shoulder. "It'll just be two or three years."

"Maybe closer to five," Bev adds. "This is quite exciting."

"I don't know why I put up with you three." Maggie scowls.

"Because you love us, that's why." Bev pulls Maggie into a side hug while she handles the camera Bo pushed on her.

I keep forgetting all of this is being recorded and possibly broadcasted to the world. Ducking my head, I try not to think about my parents watching. I can picture the vein popping out on Dad's forehead right now.

"Yeah, well, that might change," Maggie grumbles, and I cover my giggle with my hand.

This is how I picture me, Sadie, Denali, and Rory when we're older. At least, this is how I hope we'll be. I want to be getting on each other's nerves, but still thick as thieves.

"Thank you so much for helping me. This dress is incredible, and we definitely couldn't have gotten the ceremony scheduled this quick without you. You're like my very own fairy godmothers!"

Seriously, it's been less than an hour since Kemp said he'd marry me.

My toes tingle at the memory of his yes. He hadn't seemed to be pretending. Try as I might, I can't keep my hopes reined in. The memory of this day has the potential to be one that brings me great joy or pain for the rest of my life. Both will be hard to keep in the depths with the other memories.

"No, love, thank you for letting a bunch of meddling old women be a part of your special day." Sheila pats my cheek like I'm her long-lost granddaughter. "We've been rooting for you and your man since the race started. We came all the way to Vegas from Montana to have a good time and have hardly left the hotel room because we've wanted to see how you two were doing."

"The way he looks at you … mmm." Bev rubs her arms. "It just gives me the tingles."

"Really?" I guess he's doing a better job at this fake relationship than I thought.

"Oh, girl, he's head over heels in love with you," Donna says with a clap of her hands.

"Reminds me of my Donald." Maggie's smile is so sweet I want to cry, because what these women don't know is our looks are all fake.

At least, mine started out that way. Now, I'm more confused than ever. I don't want our friendship to change, but I think we've already ruined it. There's no way I can go back to the way it was when we get home.

A knock on the door with a minute warning sends a school of carp loose in my stomach.

"Okay, honey. Turn around and tell us if the old biddies did a good job." Sheila turns me to the mirror they made me keep my back to, and tears instantly blur my vision.

While the satin part stops right above the bust, sheer lace continues up to a boat neckline along my collarbones. Intricate beading adorns the lace that hugs my shoulders and back, connecting to the satin low on my back. The dress hugs my body, flaring just past my hips to a beautiful drape and train. The hem of the dress is a strikingly bright steel pink that bleeds up to pale pink-lemonade. Some trails of color lead up to my waist, while others stop above my knees. The shades of my dress and highlights in my hair remind me of the northern lights, which make the outfit even more perfect. If I would've picked my dress myself, this would have been it.

"I went ahead and bought the dress for you, honey." Maggie sniffs and dabs her eyes. "You just leave me your address, and I'll send it up to you."

"Thank you." I blink my own eyes, not wanting my mascara to run. "All of you. If we win, I'm funding your next girls' trip, and you're coming to Alaska so I can join in."

"Deal," they say in unison, then break out into laughter.

They gather around me in a rose, lavender, and vanilla hug. This moment couldn't be any more perfect.

"What are we doing wasting time?" Bev *tsks* and shoos her friends. "Let's get you married so you can win the race!"

"We'll go take our seats while you count to thirty." Donna pats my hand when we get to the Crystal Suite's door. "I've paid these nice young men to open the doors in grand style." I shake my head and open my mouth to protest, but she talks right over me. "Just because this wedding is quick doesn't mean it has to be tasteless."

They hustle in, and I count. Rubbing my hands on the gown, I shift from one foot to the other. Is this the right thing to do? The "nice young men" must've been counting because they open the doors.

Kemp's decked out in a tux with a pink vest and tie that matches the dark pink of my dress. He's fidgeting at the front of the small room next to an Elvis impersonator singing "Fools Rush In." My grin at Donna's choice of wedding officiant falters when Kemp notices me. His body stills, except for his eyes as they run from my head to my toes and back up.

When his scan reaches my gaze, his eye contact never wavers, drawing me across the short distance that separates us. He doesn't blink when he takes both my hands in his or as Elvis conducts the brief ceremony. Nor does his gaze falter when he repeats his vows. I'm so breathless by his intensity I can hardly repeat the words after Elvis myself.

There is no way this can be all for show. Right? I mean, Kemp sucks at acting, which is why we lose every time we play charades on game night.

"I now pronounce you husband and wife. Kiss the bride," Elvis proclaims, and breaks into song as our new friends cheer.

Kemp doesn't get caught up in the excitement. If anything, he savors the moment as he trails his hands up my arms, making my body tremble. His palms cup my cheeks like I'm fragile china, and I exhale a breathy sigh at how right his warm skin feels against mine.

A satisfied smile tips his mouth up a moment before he captures my lips with his. It's not the chaste peck I expected. No, this kiss melds his soul to mine, searing a path to my pounding heart and rushing an undeniable love for him through my blood.

I grab his forearms to keep from completely melting into him. He wraps his arms around my waist, and I spear my fingers through his hair just in case he tries to pull away. No other kiss has ever sparked my nerves and made me buzz with life.

An ear-piercing whistle from one of the ladies jerks us apart.

"Well, so much for not being tasteless." Donna elbows Sheila. "For goodness' sake, we aren't at a hoedown."

Kemp chuckles and shakes his head. His chest heaves against mine, his rapid heartbeat matching my own. There's a twinkle in his eyes I've never seen before.

"Well—" His voice comes out gruff and low, and he clears his throat. "You ready to win this race, Wife?"

I bite my bottom lip, loving the sound of that word directed at me.

"Absolutely, Husband."

Kemp kisses me quickly. It's like he couldn't help himself. Not that I'm complaining. Well … too much. It would've been nice if he lingered on it before pulling me out the door.

Chapter Eighteen

-*Kemp*-

My grip tightens on Violet's hand as I hail a cab outside the chapel. I'm still not convinced Violet won't regret making this decision. Yet, one look at her walking toward me down the aisle, and all doubt I wanted to marry her whooshed out the door.

I've never wanted anything as bad as I want Violet by my side forever. We definitely need to have a nice, long conversation about that when the cameras are off. I don't want her confused about whether my actions are fake or not.

"We aren't taking the car?" Violet looks down the busy street toward the parking lot.

"I don't want to risk getting lost." Plus, I just want to sit next to her for however long the ride will take, but I'm not about to let that selfish thought out. "Besides, I figure the taxi driver can navigate Vegas better than I'll ever be able to."

"Smart." She smiles up at me, and I can't help myself.

I bend down and kiss her gently as a cab stops at the curb. Opening the door, I help Violet and her dress get in, throw the packs into the trunk, then climb in next to her. Bo's already settled in the front passenger seat. The cab driver doesn't even bat an eye at the camera being shoved in his face.

"Where ya going?" He checks the side mirrors.

"Mandalay Bay as quick as you can get us," I say and buckle in.

As Violet leans over me to the women waving, I brush her hair off her shoulder and rub my thumb over the freckles there. One benefit of being on the TV show is I need to make our love convincing. In fact, it might help in me persuading Violet that we truly belong together. In real life, I wouldn't be this forward so fast, but in the pretend world, I can skip the green slope runs of the relationship and edge right into the black diamonds. Only time will tell if I have the guts to continue down the run when the cameras are off or if I hesitate and eat snow.

"Bye!" Violet hollers out the window. "Thank you!"

"Good luck, dearies," one of the women yells back.

"Remember to keep the kissing PG. The race is a family show," another adds.

"Oh, for goodness' sakes, Sheila. Get your head out of the gutter," is the last I can hear as we pull away from the curb.

Violet snickers and moves back to her seat. "Those women are amazing."

"You're amazing." I slide my hand into hers and lift it to my lips. "And beautiful."

She presses her lips together to stifle her smile and

looks out her window. How can I help her believe what I say is true? Her head snaps to the front.

"We need to go down the Strip, please." She leans forward to talk to the driver.

"That's not the fastest way to Mandalay," he counters.

"I know, but I need to see the Strip."

"All right, lady." He shrugs. "Whatever you say."

She sits back with a sigh. I lean my arm against hers, thankful Bo needed us to sit next to each other to keep us in the shot. She rests her head on my shoulder.

"Why do we need to go down the Strip?" I take my hand not clenched in hers and rub my fingertips along her wrist.

"I don't know, but I think it might be important. The clue said to keep our wits on the Strip. I figured since we haven't spent hardly anytime there, we should at least drive down. I'd hate to miss something important." She shivers, and I lean my mouth close to her ear.

"Cold?" When I whisper the question, my lips brush her ear.

"No." Her answer is breathless. She inhales deep and slow, filling her lungs full, then lets it out in a huff. "Distracted."

She glares at me, and I let loose an unrepentant smile.

"Knock it off," she scolds, but her gaze darts to my lips before she jerks it away. "We need to focus on the surroundings. Look for clues."

"Yes, ma'am." I kiss her on the cheek, then watch out the window. "Fully focused."

Thirty minutes later, the cab pulls up to the front entrance to Mandalay Bay. My eyes hurt from trying to pay attention to the passing neon lights and buildings. The exhaustion from earlier returns, and I groan as I get out of the cab.

"I know." Violet takes my hand and maneuvers her gown out of the cab. "I'm tired too."

See. We already can read each other. Another reason we're perfect for one another.

"Where do you think we need to go?" I let out a whistle as we put on our packs and rush into the hotel. "This place is enormous."

She snags a map from the check-in counter and scans it. "I don't know. There're so many places the checkpoint could be."

I look over her shoulder. What exactly did the clue say again? Something about the Bay?

"What if we start on the beach level? The clue called this place the Bay, which makes me think of water." I point to the beach stage. "Let's start here at the stage, then we can work our way around. If it's not there, I say we go to the aquarium, then the casino."

We take off through the hotel, making heads turn as we race by. We look hilarious in our fancy getups with our camping packs strapped to our backs. As wedding days go, this one has to top the charts for unique. My anxiety increases with the massive amount of people in the pool area. A good portion of them don't even have suits on, so they must be here just to watch us.

An excited kid points to the stage area where the race flags wave in the breeze. Tables with jumbles of blocks dot the decking next to the pool. Thankfully, all the tables are empty.

Violet veers to the clue box and rips it open.

The Strip of Vegas is world-renowned,
Let's hope your memory of it isn't unfurled.

"We have to do a puzzle of the Strip." She smiles, and I'm not sure if it's exhaustion or madness putting it there.

We're good at games, and she's great at mind puzzles, but my eyes crossed as we drove down the strip. I move to the table farthest from the clue just in case more teams arrive, then help Violet take her pack off. A Treasure Island hotel-shaped block snags my attention, and I blow out a huff that vibrates my lips. A line dissects the table in a wide V I'm assuming is supposed to be the Strip. Great. They cut the jumble of wood into the hotel shapes.

We are going to be here for a while.

"Let's find the Mandalay and start there." Violet digs through the blocks, lining them along the table's edge.

"But which end will it go on?" I help, my sense of uselessness rising with each piece I place in line.

"See how the tables are all east to west, not north to south?"

I survey the tables and shrug. "Sure."

"Well, the Mandalay is the last casino on the west end of the Strip. All we have to do is work backwards from there and we've got it." She glances at me as she lifts the Bay block up. "I'm so glad we took the time to drive the Strip."

"Well, time will tell how many more trips down the famous road we have to take to get it right." I know I'm grumbling, but my brain is so tired, I can't help it.

"Don't worry. This won't take too long." How in the world can she be so sure?

She places the first piece, then grabs the pyramid-shaped Luxor block. Systematically, she goes from one block to the next, only occasionally stopping to stare off into the distance. I just stand there, dumbstruck with the rest of the crowd, occasionally handing her a piece when she asks for it. When she places the Stratosphere at the opposite end and steps back to check what she did, I move next to her.

"Oh, wait." She switches the Fashion Show Mall and a hotel I can't remember the name of, then nods. "Done."

"This is so much more than a photographic memory." I look at her as the official checks the map.

Her eyes widen and dart to the crowd murmuring and shaking their heads around us. Her cheeks, rosy with victory, pale, and she swallows. For the first time, I'm thinking Will was right, and I've put Violet in a position I shouldn't have. I put my arm across her shoulder and pull her to me.

"Shh. Don't stress." I whisper into her ear and kiss her temple. "You can tell me when we get to our room."

She nods under my chin as the official whips the next clue out with a flourish.

Don't worry. You are friends, not food.

"The Shark Reef," we say in unison.

Her weary smile tugs at my heart. If there's more to the Vegas challenge, we're taking our pit stop before we continue. We've both pushed to our breaking point, plus I need to know what's going on with her. I pick up her pack and tell her I'll carry it. Her shoulders sag in relief. I'll have to remember to take her load more often, especially if all the days are full of challenges like this one has been.

We find Jill in the aquarium tunnel. Sharks swim above us, and Violet gasps in amazement. We have the Sea Life Center back home in Seward, but it has nothing like this.

"Congratulations on your wedding," Jill says as we step onto the checkpoint mat. "I'd like to add to the festivities by telling you that you are the first team to arrive."

I drop the packs and twirl Violet around.

"I have to say, I'm impressed you got all three locations done so quick." Jill's eyebrows are high on her forehead. "I'm not sure I could've done that."

"It's easy when you have the right teammate." Violet wraps her arm around my back.

I drape my arm across her shoulders and kiss her hair.

"Well, you two are definitely the team to beat." Jill hands us an envelope. "Let's see if you can keep your lead through the jungles of Central America."

I pick up our bags, and we head to check in. Hopefully, heading south means that there will be more flights between the challenges. Flights mean sleep. Sleep is good, because if all the days are at this pace, I should be worried about both of us.

Chapter Nineteen

-*Violet*-

I have never been more excited to see a hotel room door than I am at this moment. My legs weigh at least fifty pounds each, if the difficulty of lifting them is any indication. I just want to trudge into the room, fall face first onto the bed, and sleep off this exhaustion.

Too bad I owe Kemp an explanation before I can drift into dreamland.

Slipping the key into the lock, I peek back at him. He's carrying my pack again, the sweetie, and looks as tired as I feel. Truly, in all our adventures, I've never seen his eyes so tight or his shoulders drooping like they are now. He catches me staring and winks. My cheeks heat instantly, and hope stands up like the barking sea lions at the Sea Life Center when the workers come in with the fish bucket.

Bo shifts his camera next to me, making me inwardly cringe. How can I keep forgetting he's here? More importantly, how do I tell if Kemp's actions are because of the camera or because of me?

I want what my fairy godmothers said about Kemp loving me to be true with such an intensity I'm breaking out in a cold sweat. Memories thick with emotion are the hardest to keep down below the surface where they can't drag me under. If having his attention burns my soul this much, what will happen if it's all pretend, or we get home and he changes his mind?

This fear sliding up my legs like giant tentacles—tightening and wrapping—waiting to pull me under and drown me is why I've stuck to my one-kiss rule. Memories can be great. They can also destroy me, overwhelming the good until all that's left is a constant replay of the past.

The door beeps, and I push it open. Rose petals trail from the door to the king-size bed where a gift basket filled with chocolate, bubble bath, and champagne waits to be opened. Those invisible tentacles reach higher, wrapping around my waist.

A window stretches across the entire far wall where the Strip lights blink. I cross the room to stare at the view. I need to get my heartbeat and anxiety under control before I talk to Kemp, but I've never told anyone outside of my family about my H-SAM.

At first, I didn't tell because my parents didn't want me to get picked on at school. Later it stayed a secret because I didn't want others to only think about me as that chick with the crazy memory. I didn't want people to change how they acted around me because they worried I'd remember every bit of our time together.

"The network wanted to congratulate you for your wedding with the honeymoon package." Bo has said little since the race started, so it's weird hearing his voice now.

His voice strains, and I bet he's as tired as me. These camera operators are in insane shape to run all day chasing contestants while carrying all their gear. My respect for him is through the roof now, and I'm so glad he's on this adventure with us.

"Thanks." Kemp sets our packs against the wall.

I catch the bright blush climbing up his neck and press my lips together to keep from laughing. At least I'm not the only one uncomfortable right now. Bo drops the camera to the floor with a sigh.

"I'm happy for you two. Thanks for requesting me to come along. Not knowing what's going to happen is just as exciting for me as it is for you." He smiles at both of us and claps Kemp on the shoulder. "Welp. I'm tired, and you are camera free until three a.m. Get some rest." Bo winks. "Or not."

I squeeze my eyes shut and scrunch my face as he lets himself out. My cheeks burn at about a thousand degrees with embarrassment and unease. The wedding was one thing, but this whole honeymoon-suite bit is a whole new level. We might be married, but I am far from being ready for that kind of intimacy. I'm not even sure how real this marriage is.

"Praise God, today is done." Kemp crosses the room and stands next to me to peer out the window.

I'm too nervous to turn.

"It's beautiful in its own way, huh?" Kemp pushes his hands into the pockets of his tux pants, totally relaxed. "Has nothing on Alaska, our stars, and the northern lights, but Vegas will do for a night."

"Yeah."

I pull up my big girl panties and turn around. We're standing so close our arms touch. I want to wrap mine around his waist and bury myself against him.

He's made no qualms about touching me. Maybe I should take from his cue. Of course, that was when the cameras were rolling, but we've always been hugging friends. That shouldn't have to change, right? I take a deep, silent breath to fill up my courage.

"How did you know where all the pieces on the puzzle went?" Kemp's soft question deflates my bravery faster than a balloon without a knot.

My body sags under the pressure of exhaustion and nerves. I stumble back until my legs hit the edge of the bed, and I sink down onto it. Staring at the carpet, I try to slow my breaths that bottle up in my chest.

"Hey, it's okay." Kemp sits next to me, his weight making me bump against him. "You don't have to tell me if you don't want to."

My nose stings with tears, and I sniff as I look up at him.

"I … I …" I don't know if I can do this.

He rubs his hand along my shoulder. The feel of his rough skin against mine grounds me. I tuck my head under his chin and close my eyes. It shouldn't be this hard to tell him. Aside from my family, he's the most important person in my life. So why do I feel like I'm about to have my fingernails ripped out?

"Whatever you say or don't say won't change how I feel about you." Kemp's words rumble against my cheek. "I love you, Violet. You're my best friend, but it's so much more than that. You're the only one who's ever made my life brighter. Nothing will ever change that. I'd rather live without sunshine than live without you."

I snap my head up. Tears flow down my cheeks like

a glacier in summer. He wipes the pad of his thumb across my cheek, then leans forward and gently kisses me.

"We're both tired. Why don't we get some sleep?" He brushes the moisture from my other cheek, then reaches up and pulls a bobby-pin from my hair. "Life won't be so overwhelming in the morning."

My gaze darts from eye to eye, and his tiny smile softens his serious expression. He's really going to let this go? How is it I wound up fake-married to my best friend and completely flippers over fins in love?

Not that our marriage is fake.

Nope. Those documents we signed at the Clark County Marriage License Bureau are one hundred percent real. Only our intentions were pretend—at least at first.

I want this marriage, our relationship, to be real. His words make me think he wants the same. The only way we can move forward is in complete honesty.

No more pretending.

No more falsehoods.

If I want the memories of this race to be filled with the beginnings of a long, wonderful life together with Kemp, I have to trust him.

"I have hyperthymesia," I blurt out, my fingers curling around his tux jacket flaps.

His hand stills where it's pulling another pin from my hair. His eyes widen as he drags his gaze to meet mine. The tremble of his hand registers a second before he drops it to the bed, yanking some hairs with the sudden motion.

"Is it"—his Adam's apple bobs as he swallows—"terminal?"

"What?" I huff a laugh and scrunch my face in confusion.

"Is it deadly? Like a type of brain cancer or something? Is that why you can remember the hotels so well?"

Understanding floods me with humor, and I flatten my hands against his chest. His heart races against my palms.

"No, it's nothing like that. I'm not dying or even sick."

Before I can even explain, he buries his hands in my hair and ravishes my lips. This kiss has none of the tenderness of the earlier ones. It's relief and burning passion, searing all the way to my toes. His arms wrap around my back and pull me close. All those romantic expressions in all those books I've read and have been waiting for explode in my mind at once.

Fireworks boom.

Sparks sizzle.

Butterflies riot in a flutter to break loose deep in my core.

I'm floating on air and burning up at the same time.

This is what I've been longing to experience in all those first kisses. Imagine if I'd stuck to my one-kiss rule and missed out on the soul-shattering, all-consuming touch of Kemp Rees, my unintended husband.

Too quickly, he pulls away, but I wrap my fingers around his hot pink tie and hold him to me, putting all my hopes and love into my kiss. I don't want this moment to end. Forget the race. Forget life back in Alaska. I'm never leaving this hotel room again.

His low chuckle against my lips tastes delicious, like homemade hot chocolate in front of a roaring fire in winter. I sigh when he softens the kiss because I can tell he's shifting things down. When he leans away, I push my bottom lip out in a pout.

"Okay, wow." He nips my pout, sending a jolt to my belly, then leans his forehead to mine. "I guess I won't have to convince you to make this fake relationship real."

"No." I chuckle. "Guess Sawyer was right."

"Looks like we should've believed him instead of laughing it off."

"Yeah … his feelers are never wrong."

Kemp sits back and pulls another pin from my hair. "So, first off, dropping scary-sounding medical terms on your husband is a good way to an early widowhood."

"Sorry about that." I reach for my hair, but he playfully slaps my hand away.

"What exactly is hypertiemysia?"

"Hyperthymesia or H-SAM is a highly superior autobiographical memory." I pick at the comforter, suddenly nervous again. "Basically, I remember every detail of my life."

"Every detail?"

"Pretty much. My brain has the ability to pull up any event like a video and play it for me as if I'm right back there."

"Any memory? Like even childhood ones?" He finishes letting down my hair and takes my hand fiddling with the comforter in his.

Okay. Here comes the part that might freak him out.

"Some people have certain events trigger it. Some people, it's like it has always been there." I shrug, trying to downplay the way my heart is about to race out of my chest. "I can replay memories as far back as before I could crawl."

"Seriously?"

"I can't pinpoint dates or days of the week that far back, but the memories play just like the others."

My mom's face floats up from the deep, smiling down at me as I gaze up at her while I nurse. My fingers tangle in her hair. Gosh, how I loved the silky feel of it along my skin.

"It's not just memories, but actual dates and stuff?" Kemp asks.

I blink Mom's loving expression away and focus on the awe in Kemp's voice. Since the first few months after the doctor diagnosed me, I haven't really had to explain how it works. My family just accepted it and resigned themselves to me always having the past available within a matter of seconds. We figured not talking about it all the time would make it easier for me.

"Yeah. It's kind of crazy, but you ask me about a date or something that happened, and all my memories of around that time pop up, kind of like a Netflix search. When I focus in on the information I need, I can snag onto things that happened around it, and then the memories fill in like a big wall calendar of videos." I force a laugh. "I don't even know if that makes any sense or not."

"No, it makes perfect sense. I can picture it in my mind. I just can't believe my wife has superpowers like some comic hero." He pushes my hair behind my ear as a wide grin spreads across his face, flooding me with relief. "I guess I should just prepare myself to never win an argument, especially if it's about things that already happened."

"Yep." I bite my bottom lip but can't stop my mouth from stretching from ear to ear.

He's taking this much better than I thought he would. I can't believe I waited so long to tell him. Maybe keeping it a secret hasn't been the best idea? Maybe letting the world know should be the way to go? I could make it easier for other H-Sammers.

"There're a little less than a hundred people in the world diagnosed, and they aren't sure what causes it." I smooth his jacket between my fingers.

A knock on the door jerks my hand away.

"Maybe the network sent up room service to go with the bubbly." Kemp heads to the door, walking backward half the way so he can see me. "Seriously, my brain is running with questions, but I'm also exhausted. We might have to get ready for bed, then talk until we both fall asleep."

"That would be about two minutes in." With a sigh, I stand. I need to get out of this dress.

"Ivy?" Kemp opens the door wide, so Ivy and a cameraman can come in.

"Hey, guys." Her gaze darts from me to Kemp and back again. Tension lines her mouth. "We need to talk."

"Is everything okay?" I cross my arms over my chest, hating that a camera has invaded the happy moment with Kemp.

"I need to know how you finished that puzzle so fast." Ivy clears her throat. "Social media posts and the crowd at the pool are thinking you somehow cheated."

I shake my head as nausea rolls in my empty stomach. Knowing I should tell the world and actually doing it on livestream are two totally different feelings. Kemp crosses the room and takes my hand.

"Your call. Tell however much you want," he whispers before wrapping his arm around me in support and turning to Ivy.

"We didn't cheat. I just have an amazing memory." I grip Kemp's fingers on my waist. When Ivy presses her lips into a fine line of skepticism, I purge the rest of the truth out in a rush of words. "I have H-SAM. It's a rare condition where I basically remember everything that happens to me."

"Never heard of it." Ivy raises one eyebrow, and Kemp tenses next to me.

"There's very few that have it in the world, but that actress Marilu Henner from the old TV show *Taxi* does."

"I remember watching a documentary on that." The cameraman tips his head to the side to see around his equipment. "You actually have that? Like you can remember dates and what day of the week stuff happened?"

"Yeah." My laugh is short and full of relief.

"Wicked cool." Hearing a middle-aged man say that phrase relaxes me even more.

"Most of the time." I lean into Kemp, more exhausted than ever before.

Who knew baring one's soul would be this taxing?

"Can we verify this?" Ivy takes out her phone and taps on the screen.

"Quiz her about an event," the cameraman suggests. "Who won the Oscar for Best Actor in a Leading Role in 2012?"

"It doesn't work that way." I shake my head in frustration. I shouldn't get upset because he's just trying to help me. I'm just tired. "H-SAM stands for Highly

Superior Autobiographical Memory. I could care less about Oscars and whatnot, so I won't have any memory of it."

Ivy shifts and tilts her head to the side. "What day did the earthquake hit Anchorage in 2019?"

"November 30th. It was a Saturday, and the earthquake struck at 8:29 in the morning. I was still in my You Otter Be Reading pjs." I look up at Kemp. "You know the ones with an otter floating on his back, holding a book?"

"I remember those." Kemp nods, his small grin encouraging.

"Anyway, I was eating yogurt with frozen salmonberries I'd picked that summer when my stomach felt like I was getting motion sickness, and the dresses I had hanging on the string stretched over the wood stove started swaying. I laughed because it looked like they were dancing without me in them. We'll get earthquakes now and then, so I didn't think much of it. Thirty minutes later, I got a call from Dad saying they needed Search and Rescue up in Anchorage to help make sure no one was trapped where the most damage was. Thankfully, no one died." I suck in a breath and force a laugh. "I'm sorry. You didn't ask for all of that. The earthquake happened Saturday, November 30th."

Ivy looks up from her phone. "Okay. If I need more than this, is there someone I can call?"

"Yeah. I can give you my parents' number. They have all my diagnostic paperwork from my doctor appointments." I roll my eyes. "They kept everything, like some kind of trophy or something."

"That should work." Ivy lowers her phone. "I'll let

you know before your flight if the network is okay with you continuing on the race."

"That's not—"

"Okay." I squeeze Kemp's hand and talk over him.

"Congratulations on your wedding." Ivy gives us her first genuine smile, then heads to the door.

"You okay?" Kemp wraps his other arm around me, hugging me close.

"Yeah."

He kisses the skin just above my collar on my shoulder. "I'm ordering whatever food they can deliver fast, then we are sleeping. My questions can wait."

I nod against his neck, though, with the worry of what the network will say, I doubt I'll be able to sleep. I squeeze my eyes tight and release the future and unknown to tomorrow. If I'm going to be ready to race, I'm going to need all the sleep I can get. Besides, whatever the network decides won't matter in the long run, not when leaving the race with Kemp as my husband makes me a winner either way.

Chapter Twenty

-*KEMP*-

The older woman sitting next to me in the converted school bus bumps into me for the hundredth time. She can't help it, not with how us passengers are stuffed into the Guatemalan chicken bus like circus clowns. Every time the driver pulls to a stop, I'm sure he's going to say there's no more room. He doesn't, and now I'm squished between a woman holding an oversized, tightly woven basket that keeps squawking and Violet bent over her art notebook. I'd have her sit on my lap to get more space, but I'm worried someone else will just squeeze into the seat with us.

Watching Violet draw in her notebook while jostling along the rugged mountain road fascinates me. I wouldn't be able to make a straight line with the bumpy ride, let alone the intricate drawing she's creating with nothing but a pack of colored pencils. If the ride was smooth, the noise from the overcrowded, noisy interior would distract me.

For the first hour and a half of the ride, she had her

face glued to the window, inhaling every sight with her eyes. About an hour ago, she pulled out her art supplies from her small bag and only occasionally looked up. Is that because she's on memory overload? Maybe one of the "processing" issues Will warned about? There is so much I want to ask her, but I don't want my questions to seem like an interrogation. And there's also the camera trained on us to worry about. If only she would've told me before, then we wouldn't have to worry about what the entire world heard.

There is so much that we need to talk about, but both of us were so exhausted last night that we fell asleep almost instantly. Then, once we got the green light to go, we've had our trusty cameraman filming our every interaction. Makes talking about things like her H-SAM and our future impossible.

In fact, once we boarded the plane, the questions I was at first too excited and then too exhausted to think about sprang up. What will we do once snowboarding season starts again? I'm gone most of the winter. Is it right to ask her to leave her family and the kennel just so I can play in the snow? Granted, my playing makes me lots of money, but is that the kind of life she wants? Is it what I want for my family?

And speaking of family, what is hers going to think? They've always treated me as one of their own, but that was before I eloped with their daughter. I doubt that's the kind of "taking care of" Will was talking about.

She's drawing two hands again. It's similar to the painting in her studio back home that she'd created the day I asked her to marry me. That artwork had all kinds of dreary feelings welling up in me to combine with my proposal anxiety. This one bursts with vividness and emotion. Instead of each hand being dominated by a color tone, both hands swirl red, blue, and purple with some yellow and orange thrown in. It's harmonious in its typical Violet style and leaves me with a sense of hope and love, maybe even comfort.

A man stands on the side of the road up ahead, waving his hat in the air. The bus slows, and I groan. At this rate, it'll take us the rest of the afternoon and night to get to Panajachel. If the challenge is like at Moab, we'll have to wait until tomorrow to do it, which will give other teams time to catch up.

Shifting in my seat, I huff out my frustration and think about how thankful I am that we're on the bus at all. I still can't believe we made it to the bus terminal. Honestly, if the college student we sat next to on the plane from Dallas hadn't ridden in the taxi there with us, we might have completely walked past the "terminal." (Really, it was just a green and beige bus parked along the street across from a bright blue shop. Not what I would consider a terminal.)

The man on the road climbs up the stairs, making the woman sitting next to me squish me more. The basket screeches and jerks in the woman's hands. Violet snaps her head up as I stop the basket from toppling on us, slapping the lid back in place.

"Gracias." The woman beams at me.

"¿Qué hay allí?" I hope I'm asking what's in her basket and not something else. It's been several years since my high school Spanish class.

"Me pollitos preciosos." She pats the basket of chickens affectionately, then peeks at the driver and back at me. "Shh. No se supone que esté aquí."

I'm pretty sure she just said she's not supposed to

have them in here. A few other passengers had cages with chickens, and they're up on the top of the bus with the baggage. I place my index finger to my lips and then zip across my mouth. She chuckles, covering her mouth with her hands.

She talks rapidly with the woman in the seat across the aisle, grabs a bundle from her, then passes it to me. "Here. For you. Eat."

I unwrap the bright fabric to find three half-circle pastries. "Empanadas?"

"Sí."

"Gracias." I nod and smile at her and hand one to Violet and another over the seat to Bo. I don't know if it's against the race rules since we aren't supposed to interact with him, but the man has to eat.

"Oh, these smell delicious." Violet holds one up to her nose and sniffs. "Thank you."

The woman goes back to talking with her friend, so I point to Violet's notebook. "Never thought someone could make art like that with colored pencils."

Violet leans her head on my shoulder as she takes a bite of the pastry. "It's how I process the day, kind of like a journal. When I was younger and we finally understood why I had all these memories jumbling up my brain, my dad suggested I write things down. He thought putting them on paper might help me sort them."

"Smart man." I capture a whiff of her shampoo and breathe it in. "Did it help?"

"I wasn't much for writing, but I loved art. So, at the end of the day, I started doing drawings of the events that wanted the most attention. It seems to help me process the day and push the memories down. Eventually, I got really good at art." She sits up and wags her eyebrows at me.

I miss her leaning against me, but the sun flickering through the windows onto her face makes it worth it. Man, this amazing woman is my wife. Mine. It's hard to believe possible.

I clear my throat as I think back to her house. "All those paintings in your cabin are memories?"

"Yeah. Mostly. Some are just for fun. I have notebooks like this filled with them too." She rubs her hands over the picture, and it's then I see her engagement ring on one hand.

So, the painting is of our hands? This is what being together makes her feel?

"Be warned. We may need a room just to hold them all by the time we get old."

I love that she's talking about us growing old together, even if I have a million questions and doubts swirling in my head.

"Baby, I'll build you a whole separate studio if that's what you want."

"Really?"

"Yep. Two-stories with enormous windows so you can look outside and an entire second floor just to put your memories."

Her expression turns serious, and she places a lingering kiss on my lips. For someone with a one kiss rule, she is amazingly good at this. Dropping the empanada in my lap, I dive my fingers into her hair. I don't care that the entire world might be watching. I'm taking the time to show my wife that she makes my life vibrant and bursting with color too.

The bus hits a bump. Our seat partner gasps a

moment before the basket knocks hard into my back. Wings, feet, and joyous clucking assault my face as the "pollitos preciosos" make a break for it. Violet half shrieks, half laughs as she saves one from bailing out the open window. Hands and shouts reach from over the seat to help capture the birds.

I snag one as it attempts to fly over Bo's head. He's laughing so hard I'm surprised the camera isn't bobbing up and down. The bird tries to jolt from my hands, and I almost let it when I finally look at the thing.

These aren't your run-of-the-mill chickens. Nope. This bad boy looks like a member of some eighties hard-rock band with the way his black and rust-colored feathers stick straight out of his head.

"Oh, Pedro." The woman grabs the chicken, makes a *tsking* noise at him, then shoves him in the basket.

After five minutes of squawking, and her scolding each by name, the chickens are snuggled in their basket. All the other passengers go back to talking like poultry exploding into the bus in a flurry of feathers is an everyday occurrence. Maybe it is, because as I settle in, I realize the driver never once swerved off course.

Fifteen minutes, and a lot of stifled laughter from me and Violet later, we empty off the bus with the other passengers. The town of Panajachel sits on the shores of Lake Atitlán and is gorgeous.

It's also swarming with people.

I hail a yellow taxi to take us to the Calle Santander. I'm not taking the chance of getting lost, especially with the way the sky is showing signs of sunset. We have to make up time from the long bus ride. When the taxi pulls to a stop, two other teams are racing down the brightly colored market street.

I knew it.

Any lead we had from getting married has vanished.

Will Violet regret the move since it seems it didn't help?

"Come on." She grabs my hand and pulls me after them.

The only good thing about there being teams ahead of us is we don't have to look too hard for the clue. We rush up behind the basketball team as they snag theirs. A man dressed in Mayan clothing hands us a bright orange envelope like the ones the other two teams are already bending over.

Adventure or Culture?

Violet reads the clue aloud.

"That's it?" I crane my neck to read the paper.

"Culture. Culture. Please. Please. Please." Violet squishes her palms together and dances from foot to foot, making her begging even more adorable.

"I don't know." I grit my teeth and tilt my head from side to side in consideration. "Adventure might be easier."

"Adventure!" The basketball team isn't quiet in their whispering.

The man hands them a red envelope. Tyrone claps me on the shoulder as he rushes away. The Marshpillow siblings don't even hide their "adventure" choice. Indecision wars within me. If we make another mistake, we might never make up the gap.

"Please." Violet bites her lower lip, gripping her fingers together under her chin. And I'm pretty sure I'm doomed to a life full of giving in with that look.

"Okay." I sigh and shake my head. "Culture it is."

Her cheers have those gathering around to watch laughing, and she kisses me quickly before turning to the man with the clues. She even gives him a peck on the cheek, making the old man's dark face blush darker and the crowd to clap loudly. By the end of this race, I'll be surprised if the world isn't as wild about Violet as I am.

She rips open the clue and reads:

Color and culture abound in Santa Catarina Palopó.
Get ready for an enlightening experience for all the senses.

"¿Donde es el Hotel Villa Santa Catarina?" She reads from the back of the clue and scans the crowd for help.

"Vamos." A little boy grabs her hand and pulls her down the street.

Violet looks back at me, her face wide with joy as she points her thumb at her helper. Bringing her was the best choice I ever made.

Ever.

The boy keeps Violet's hand tightly in his as he leads us through the crowds. When we make it out of the market, he talks rapidly to a man with a Toyota truck decked out with metal bars along the bed and benches in the back. The man motions for us to get into the bed of the vehicle. Since I heard the boy mention Santa Catarina, I'm assuming we aren't being stolen away. The camera setup with wi-fi and broadcasting our location adds to my sense of security, but I climb in before Violet, just in case.

The truck bumps down the two-lane road, wind rushing to tangle and blow Violet's hair into both our faces. She pulls the rubber band from her hair and tries to gather it back together. The truck swerves, and she almost falls off the bench.

"Here, let me." I grab the band from her and smooth her hair back.

It's not the best bun ever, and might not hold, but something about the intimacy of the action has me leaning close and pressing my lips to the now exposed skin of her neck. She turns from scanning the green mountains that climb from the lake and gives me a small smile. The driver's music blares in a festive, upbeat tempo so loudly from the cab, I can barely hear Violet's "Thank you." I nod my reply, then point over her shoulder as a town comes into view.

"Oh, Kemp," Violet exclaims at the brightly painted houses. "Look at the patterns!"

The houses and buildings dotting the mountainside have been decorated in bright colors with traditional Guatemalan patterns and symbols incorporated in the designs. They're hard to make out in the fading light, so I hope we're still here in the morning to see it during the day. I chuckle at myself. Thirty minutes ago, I thought we might have made the slower choice in challenges, and now I want to stay here longer? I keep this up, and we might come in dead last.

Violet spins back to me, takes my cheeks in her hands, and sears my lips with a kiss that has my hairs standing on end.

"Thank you for doing this challenge." She pulls back as the truck stops. "I don't even know what it is, but this moment, with the brilliant sunset lighting the lake on fire, these beautiful houses like jewels darting the mountainside, and you here with me will be a memory I'll savor for the rest of my life."

Yep. I'm a goner. I can't even respond past the lump in my throat. I kiss her cheek and pull her into a hug before helping her out of the truck.

I don't care if we win the race. Heck, I don't even care if we finish. I'm not even sure I care where we live or what we do. One thing is painfully clear. My goal for the rest of my life, until the day I die, is to give this woman so many happy memories that all the others get drowned in the abundance.

Chapter Twenty-One

-Violet-

I squeeze Kemp's hand as we walk down the street along the lake to the school. This morning when the clue slid under our door, I almost didn't want to open it. The sun rising over the mountains put on another spectacular show, splashing colors through the floor-to-ceiling windows and over the bed where Kemp had been eating breakfast.

It's more than a little weird waking up next to your best friend only to realize he's now your husband. I can't quite get a handle on what he's thinking. I know we should talk about the future, about what will happen when the race is over. It's why I'm glad we haven't let anything go past kissing. Honestly, I just want the bubble of happiness to just remain, at least a little bit longer.

I definitely didn't want to leave that peaceful moment in the room, eating tropical fruit and drinking Guatemalan coffee, but my drive to win this race won out. I'm compromising by making him walk to the next challenge so I can gorge on the painted houses nestled in this quaint village.

"What do you think the challenge will be?" Kemp points at a fishing boat trolling out on the lake. "Hopefully, it's fishing. That's cultural, right?"

"That could be fun, but I don't think kids would be involved with that."

The clue held two words like the day before. Abuelas or niños. While I'd love to spend more time with women like our seat partner on the bus, doing something that involved children tugged at my heart.

Probably would every time.

A group of kids waits in front of the school, running toward us when we get close. Some are in traditional dresses of beautifully woven fabric. While others dress like the kids back home. Their small hands pull on mine to hurry. Little faces hold so much happiness, it bubbles up into me.

They lead us around the back to an open yard with basketball hoops. Large trees shade the dirt area. I can see the lake meeting the mountain beyond. There's not any grass in the expanse of dirt, but it still reminds me of Waterfront Park back home.

The kids lead us to a young woman about our age dressed in a bright Guatemalan dress, their gazes bouncing between the adults like popcorn.

"Welcome to Santa Catarina Palopó." The woman smiles at us. "My name is Rosa, and I'm what you would call the principal here. My students and I are pleased you have picked this challenge."

The kids cheer, and I am so glad Kemp agreed to the culture challenge, even though adventure will always be more up his alley. The principal motions to two-by-four frames, probably seven feet by twenty feet in size. Big plastic tubs line the area next to the frames. My eyes widen as memories of a research paper I did in middle school rush to the surface.

"Every year during Semana Santa, before Easter and feria celebrating our patron saint Santa Catarina de Alejandria in November, we make alfombras as a celebration of the sacrifice of Jesus for our sins and to honor our saint," Rosa explains, and I'm so glad we chose culture.

"Oh, I did a research paper about this in geography." I clap my hands together in excitement.

"Of course, you did." Kemp rolls his eyes.

"The alfombras are made from dyed sawdust, pine needles, flowers, fruit … basically anything natural that we can create a beautiful offering with." Rosa shrugs. "It's important for us that our children learn this tradition, so we always encourage them to participate. They will be here to answer questions if you need them, and we have examples of alfombras the children created hanging on the school. You must complete an alfombra that is beautiful and honors your beliefs. We have stencils you can use, and you can work with any supplies offered here. When you are done, the children will vote on whether your alfombra passes the standard expected for such an offering."

Oh, this is a challenge I'll relish. We go to the wall where pictures of past alfombras hang. The kids point to the ones they did, and I ooh and ahh way too long, if Kemp's shifting from foot to foot is any indication. The artwork these kids created takes my breath away, and I just hope we can create something that will meet the high standard.

I move to the supplies we have to create with, letting the thick aroma of cleansing pine, heady flowers, and sweet fruits saturate my senses. The bright colors of the dyed sawdust speak of the vibrant people. It screams a joy and deep connection to their past that explodes into the paint of their buildings and threads woven in their clothing.

Dipping my hand in a tub of dark, blue-dyed sawdust, I stare at the frame. How do I honor this amazing culture while marrying it with mine? I look out past the fence surrounding the yard, reminded again how similar Seward and Santa Catarina Palopó are, despite being thousands of miles apart. I think of the beauty of my home, the love and support of my family, and our church community that will drop everything to help someone in need.

I look at the man next to me, kicking a ball back and forth with two boys. He works so hard to be better than how he was raised, has accepted me and my uniqueness without a second thought, and shown me that love is more than tingling while kissing. It's friendship, respect, communication, and trust. A picture forms in my head of what I want the alfombra to look like. I might be biting more off than we can chew, but together, Kemp and I can do it.

"I've got a plan." I grab a bowl from a girl and scoop it into the pungent sawdust.

It would take too long to explain it to Kemp, so I just start ordering him around. Working with the sawdust, while more difficult than paint, is just as satisfying. The heavy smell surrounds us like it does when we hike back home, which just feeds into my creativity. For the next two hours, poor Kemp races back and forth, bringing supplies and snapping to my commands like some frazzled artist's assistant. Another two teams arrive, and I force myself not to rush. This needs to honor not only the Guatemalan culture but our own.

An hour later, the tennis team hollers they're done. Disappointment rushes cold to my fingers as I let the bright teal sawdust run through my hands on to our alfombra. Kemp must be frustrated with how long this is taking. I sit up on my knees on the two-by-six stretched across the frame so I can work on the middle and look over at the other team's work.

Heat races up my neck as I glare at what they've created. They've just dumped sawdust into the frame and put some flowers in a pattern. Not only is it sloppy work, but it's a slap in the face to all the hard work and intricate designs the children and people of this village create each year. The kids aren't shy about their disapproval, booing and giving two thumbs down while shaking their heads.

"I told you we should've done adventure." One of the team members tosses a large flower into the frame, sending sawdust flying.

"They need to show a little respect," Kemp growls as he hands me more sawdust.

"Yeah, but I don't think they're making a favorable impression on the judges." I point my chin to a group of girls huddled with their arms crossed, glaring at the tennis team. "These niños won't let them slide."

I'm almost finished with our alfombra. Though I wish I could spend time putting in more details, the race begs for us to at least attempt to hurry. My knees and back ache as I stand. Kemp helps me walk across the board to the side, then lifts the board from the frame. I scan the picture we've created as I walk around it, searching for anything that needs fixing.

"It's beautiful." Kemp's awe-filled voice stops me next to him and switches my perusal to a less critical one.

Kemp's boat points out to sea near the bottom of the frame. Behind it, the lights of Seward dot along a dark mountainside and reflect off the ocean. A full moon lights a path in the ocean for the boat and dissipates in a fading trail behind. The lantern shining from the boat intersects with the light from the moon to make a cross. Northern lights dance in the sky, splashing color onto the ocean. Two people hold hands at the bow of the boat.

"Oh, this is a marvilloso tribute." Rosa places her hands on her cheeks as her wide eyes take in the alfombra.

"It's our story, how God's love can be seen in the wake of our past and is guiding our future even in the darkness." I point to the moonlight on the ocean.

Rosa turns to the children gathered around chattering. "Niños, qué crees?"

Cheers and clapping explode like parrots taking flight in the jungle. The kids throw thumbs up and hug us with such exuberance, tears stream down my cheeks. Bo takes out his phone and snaps pictures with one hand while continuing to film with the other while Rosa hands us the next clue.

"You'll have to send me that." Kemp points to Bo, then pulls me close, whispering in my ear. "Thank you. While nothing can top the last challenge, this one comes close."

He kisses my hair, my face heating for a completely different reason. I clear my throat and open the clue.

Rio is more than just a carnival. So, come and learn its breadth. After the mountains of Guatemala, get ready to discover the depths.

"We're going to Brazil," I whisper-scream to Kemp.

I don't want to give the other two teams any idea where we are going. Though, by the looks of their alfombras, they'll be here a while. As Kemp high-fives kids on our way out, I take one last look at the sawdust painting. When we get home, I'm painting a huge copy of it and hanging it in our living room, whoever's house that will be at.

Chapter Twenty-Two

I scan the gate our flight is supposed to take off from, and inwardly groan at the three teams already there. The basketball team and another team sit off to one side, laughing and talking loudly. The Marshpillow siblings sit on the opposite side of the waiting area, glaring across the seats. I head to the basketball team. I want no more drama than we already have.

I turn to find Violet surrounded by Guatemalans praising her alfombra. It's been like that since we left the school, and it's the one downfall to this race being broadcast live. It's good that the people are grateful for how she honored their culture with her art. If it had been up to me, we would have skipped the experience altogether and gone for the adventure. But the way Violet's shoulders slope and the weariness in her smile screams she needs a break. I just don't know if she'll get it here.

"Hey, baby, we're right over here." I gently push my

way through her fans and wrap my arm around her waist. "Gracias. Adiós."

I'm not sure if that's the right thing to say, but it's all I can come up with. I pull Violet to an open seat with the others. Most people stay away from the cameras, or at least hover in the peripheral, so hopefully being with the other teams will dissuade a crowd and give Violet a break.

Tyrone introduces us to Matt and Sally Hillman, the Nascar driver and his wife. Their southern accent is so thick it almost makes me miss Louisiana. Actually, being on the race, I've missed Louisiana more than I have since I left. Granted, it's the food and atmosphere I miss, not my family and so-called friends.

"Yo, why is it we all stink like we've bathed in sweat, then rolled in something nasty, and you two smell like you belong in some commercial for a woodsy perfume?" Tyrone sniffs Violet as she sits next to him. "Seriously, we picked the wrong challenge."

"Oh, it was incredible," Violet gushes, then spends the next ten minutes talking about Santa Catarina Palopó.

They lean into the story, captured by her descriptions of the village, the kids, and the alfombra. I can almost feel the sawdust in my hands again. Maybe I'll have to take Violet back, really explore the streets and visit with the locals. If we timed it right, she could watch the residents create their own alfombras.

Of course, both celebrations take place during my snowboarding season. I never have time for trips then. That thought circles me back to my doubts. Shoot, I don't even know how me being gone half the year will work. Will Violet come with me to the training base in

Utah? What about when I travel? There's no way she'll be willing to leave her family. Right? I stare at her like I'll find the answers just by looking. I can't ask her now, not with the cameras running.

"Man, you got to play with sawdust and flowers while we spent the most grueling twenty-four hours climbing a volcano."

"Really?" Violet's gaze bounces from one to the other. "That's cool."

"No. No, it wasn't." Matt shakes his head.

"It was hot and steep and hot. Did I mention that?" Tyrone's teammate, Michael, flops back in his chair. "I've been through rough trainings before, but nothing compared to that."

"I told you we should've done culture." Sally smacks Matt on the shoulder. "But nooo, 'culture sucks.'"

"I never said that." Matt's defense dies as Sally's eyebrow rises in challenge.

"Not all the teams enjoyed it as much as we did." I shrug. "The tennis team threw a fit when their first attempt didn't pass inspection."

"Oh, I don't doubt it." Sally *tsks* then leans forward like she's getting ready to give us juicy gossip. "Last year at the Open, the blond one, Sergei, slammed his racket against the fencing post when they lost. Broke it in half."

"Those kids let him have it." I laugh, remembering their faces. "They won't go easy on them now."

"I'm going to go to the restroom and clean up a bit." Violet grabs her bag and hefts it to her shoulder with a grunt.

"I'll join you." Sally quickly follows.

As soon as they are out of earshot, Tyrone punches me in the shoulder. "You two seriously got married?"

"Yeah." I rub my arm. "Seemed like a good idea at the time."

"Whatever wins the race." Michael chuckles. "Wish I had a convenient solution like that in my pocket."

"It's not like that." Except it really was. Our entire relationship is exactly like that.

"Sure." Michael rolls his eyes.

"There was a time I wanted to elope with Sally. Weddings are brutal, especially southern weddings with big families." Matt shivers. "I never imagined my Sally would turn into Bridezilla, but she did."

"After our trek on the volcano, I can imagine. Am I right?" Tyrone high fives Michael, then holds his hand up for Matt.

"Yeah. Okay, but normally she's a sweetie." Matt returns the high five with a laugh, then turns to me. "Marriage isn't easy, man."

"I know." My parents' relationship proves that.

"Marriage in our field of work makes it ten times harder." Matt motions between the four of us. "Our jobs will pull us away from family all season and wedges itself in off-season. Sure, it's all fun when it's just the two of you. It's easy for her to tag along, but once she pops out babies, it's not so much fun."

I hadn't thought that far ahead. What do I know about family and raising kids? I was alone most of my life, even when my parents were around. And when they deemed it necessary to engage, it was only to tear me down and mold me into the perfect image of a son.

"I'd suggest taking time to really talk about your plans for the future now, so you both aren't disappointed." Matt shrugs and sits back as Violet and Sally return.

Can I put Violet through a marriage where my job takes me away? I've never really thought of snowboarding as a job. It's always been fun, a passion, but never a job. Until now. Do I want to take the joy of the sport away for worry over how it tears me from my family?

I clench my teeth and stare out the window at the planes coming and going. I want what's best for Violet. Maybe what's best for her would be going through with the original plan and breaking things off when we get back.

She threads her hand through mine and leans on my shoulder with a sigh. I kiss her on the top of the head, my throat tight with the thought of giving her up. If that's what will make her happy in the long run, I'll do it. It'll rip my heart from my chest, but I'll do it.

Chapter Twenty-Three

-Violet-

I scan the beautiful coastline of the main island of Brazil's volcanic archipelago, called Fernando de Noronha. The travel dossier we received for this leg of the race claimed this area has some of the most gorgeous tropical landscapes in South America. With my family's love of going to Hawaii in the winter, I've always dreamed of traveling to places like this.

Have I been able to immerse myself in the surrounding beauty? To the vibrant culture that greeted us at the airport?

Nope.

Not one bit.

And it's only partly because of traveling the last twenty-plus hours from Guatemala City to San Jose, Panama to Rio de Janeiro to Sao Paulo Congonhas to finally make it to Fernando de Noronha. Mostly it's because of the big lug sitting next to me who spent the entire trip not talking to me.

Well, not talking past his dumb "Are you cold?" or

"Want me to find you some food?" My lips twitch, wanting to smile at how he looks after me. I school the happy grin from taking over. I'm not about to let his sweetness overshadow his distance. My family may give me a hard time for not being able to stay angry, but this time I'm going to … probably.

I turn and glare at Kemp's profile. Maybe if I stare long enough, he'll acknowledge that I know something is up and actually talk. His neck reddens, but he continues to watch the coastline pass. Oh, he's good, but I'm better. I shift my entire body so it's facing him. When he finally peeks over at me, I lift one eyebrow and cross my arms over my chest.

"What?" He chuckles, but I know Kemp. That laugh is as fake as the Marshpillow sister's eyelashes.

"You ready to tell me what's going on?" I lean close so the cameras' microphones hopefully won't pick up our conversation.

"Nothing's going on. I'm just tired." He darts his gaze to the other contestants on the boat, then reluctantly looks back at me.

"That may be the truth, but that's not what I'm talking about, and you know it." I practically hiss the last part.

"And you think now is a good time to chat about things?" He pointedly looks at the other contestants and the cameras.

"Well, you had twenty hours of travel time without the audience." I flop back in the seat. The world is probably eating up this lover's spat.

He leans over, his lips brushing my ear. I shiver at the touch despite being madder than a mama grizzly.

This does not bode well for my ability to stay angry and make him talk.

"Wilde, there's just a lot to think about." His use of my last name, like he did back when we were just friends, tangles nerves in my stomach.

Kemp leans his forehead against the side of my head and huffs out a weary sigh. "Can we talk later, please?"

I melt like ice cream next to a wood stove. "Okay."

Great. Even with the ability to remember the past perfectly, I'm never going to win in an argument with Kemp. Not that I really care about winning, at least not in that sense.

"All right, folks. Are you ready to dive for sunken pirate treasure?" José, our guide for the challenge, claps his hands together in excitement as the boat motor stops.

"No way." Tyrone high fives Michael.

"I'm not a very good swimmer." Sally, who has spent the entire boat ride wringing her hands, looks at Matt like she's going to throw up.

"No worries, señora." José waves off the concern. "We have two different levels. Shallow snorkeling." He motions toward the little island's sandy beach where flags mark sections. "And deep diving." He points the opposite direction where buoys bob in the water. "You choose your adventure."

Kemp and I turn to each other and, without hesitation, say, "Dive."

Mad or not, I can't keep the smile that spreads across my lips under control this time. We make our way to the assistant helping with diving gear, and five minutes later, I'm swimming in the clearest water I think

I've ever seen. Whatever we're searching for should be easy here.

The warm water relaxes the tension in my muscles. When we get to the pink-flagged section assigned to us, we dive. Right outside our buoys, a large ship lies on its side. Coral covers the hull, and bright fish dart in and out of the holes busted in the wood.

The front of the ship catches my attention, so I swim toward it. On the bow of the ship, a figurehead still gazes across the water. The ocean has worn the finish, and the wood shows significant deterioration, but I can make out the image of a long-haired mermaid. Her tranquil face beckons me to explore the sea with her.

A touch on my shoulder startles me, releasing a cascade of bubbles in front of my mask. Kemp shakes his head, his eyes shining in amusement through his goggles. I may still be upset at him for not talking to me, but I don't want that to distract me from the amazing beauty of this place. He tips his head to the roped area and motions me to follow.

I take the metal detector to one corner while Kemp goes to the other. The crew buried sixteen coins somewhere in this square that we need to find to move on. The area is enormous, probably twenty-by-forty feet. Searching the ocean floor will take forever, and the potential to miss a coin is high. I need to be one hundred percent on if we want to get this challenge done today. If we don't finish before the sun goes down, finding them at night will take even longer.

As I turn on the metal detector, I chuckle at the clicking noise it makes, like some kind of alien creature. I hope the camera attached to my goggles picks that up and makes someone on the other side of the screen smile. As I scan it across the sand, the woo-woo-wooing signaling metal picks my heartbeat into a run. I tuck the detector under my arm and dig, using the small wand detector the crew member gave me to zero in on the location.

Whatever's hiding here is deep. Sand clouds my vision, but I keep digging. The wand's loud buzz says it's here. Finally, my fingers rub against a round, flat coin. I hold it up to my face, surveying the intricate design on the face.

"Wahoo!" I hold my hands up in victory, though no one can hear me.

I look over at Kemp, but he's so focused he doesn't notice. Placing the coin in the pouch hanging at my side, I make sure it's sealed tight before I search again. An hour and fifteen minutes later, I check my oxygen and head over to Kemp. I tap his oxygen monitor and head to the boat.

"How many have you found?" he asks the instant he breaks the surface and rips off his mask.

"Six." I breathe in the salty scent of the ocean and close my eyes to the heat of the sun warming my face. "You?"

"Seven."

"Really?" My eyes pop open. "We're only three away."

"Yeah, but it can still take us hours to find those three."

Geesh, his optimism is infectious. I roll my eyes and swim to the boat. After a quick snack, drink of water, and an update on the other teams getting new tanks, I'm back in the water more encouraged than when I got out. We've found five more than Tyrone and Michael, seven more than the Hillmans. Hopefully, we can keep the lead and get the first ride back to town.

Three hours and one more tank of air later, my hope is waning like the sunlight. I should head up for more air, but I want to finish this pass to the border. Just as I'm about to the end, the woo-woo sound floats up to me. After four and a half hours of this, I know not to get my hopes up. I have just as many bottle caps and smashed cans in my pouch as I do coins. I dig, ignoring the warning alarm my oxygen monitor beeps … again.

My fingers graze across a round object, but my shoulders slump at the wrong size. Just another bottle cap. At this rate, it'll take us all night to find the last coins.

Kemp taps on my shoulder and points up. I nod, and he takes off for the surface. As I go to follow, the detector signals again, just to the left of where I'd just dug.

I glance at my oxygen monitor.

There's enough for one more spot.

I dig with a vengeance, careful not to throw whatever is buried away with the sand. The wand beeps every time I put it up to the floor, so I keep at it. My oxygen monitor blares a warning, but this time it doesn't stop.

Kemp's back, and he pulls on my arm. I shake him off and keep digging. The surface isn't that far away. Even if I run out of oxygen, I can make it to the top. Kemp pulls again, but I push him away, handing him my larger detector so all I have to worry about is the wand.

I'm almost to the metal. Just a little deeper and I'll be there.

My oxygen stops flowing, so I hold my breath and keep digging. Kemp's hand wraps around my bicep in a grip I won't be able to break just as my fingers skim metal. I kick toward the ocean floor as Kemp tries to drag me up. I fumble with the item, but finally clench it in my palm.

The instant we break the surface, Kemp is on me. "Are you nuts?"

"Just got the gold fever." I say between sucking for air.

"No treasure is worth you dying."

"Please, we weren't far from the surface." I wipe the water from my face. "Besides, it was worth it."

I hold up the gold coin with an enormous smile.

"Wahoo!" Kemp splashes me, causing me to sputter. "We have all sixteen."

Five minutes later, we wave goodbye to the other teams. I flop into a seat. Kemp sits on the other side of the boat with a sigh, his gaze brushing over me before it darts away. All the effervescent bubbles of victory coursing through my veins pop in one deflating whoosh.

Chapter Twenty-Four

-*Kemp*-

As the raft splashes over another rapid, I clench my hands around the paddle and dig into the water. I glance over at Violet to make sure she's okay. Her mouth is open in a smile that stretches from ear to ear. A wave crashes over her, drenching her from head to toe, but she comes out with her grin even wider.

I shake my head and focus on the Urubamba River in the Peruvian rain forest near Machu Picchu just as the raft dips and a swell covers me. The best thing about the pace of this leg is how I've been able to avoid Violet's questions. We both crashed on the overnight flights from Rio de Janeiro to Santiago to Lima. Thankfully, talking in the rental car with the camera shoved in our faces is as unappealing to Violet as it is to me. Eventually, there will be a mandatory pit stop, and I won't be able to put off talking to her any longer.

The only problem is I don't know what my problem is.

I know … confusing.

It's been hard to concentrate on the tasks at hand with my doubts circling like vultures. The raft lurches over a rapid, almost throwing me from the seat.

"Kemp, pay attention!" Violet's reminder isn't needed, or it shouldn't be.

Apparently, careening over raging rapids isn't enough to tear my thoughts from whether or not annulling my marriage is the right choice.

"Sorry." For everything.

But I leave the last bit off.

I don't want to ruin this experience for her with my brooding. We take the next rapid at an angle that crashes my side of the raft against a boulder. At the last second, I pull the paddle in and avoid my arm getting smashed.

The rapids smooth to mellow water as quickly as they descended to chaos. I slump back with a huff. We've already gone through several of these series. How many more could there possibly be?

"If you want to take a swim or have a snack before the next rapids, now is the time." Diego, our guide, nods at us, and I groan.

It's not very manly or in line with my extreme snowboarding image. I could care less at this point. Exhaustion hangs so heavy on me from the constant go and my worrying about what to do after the race, that if I look like a wimp, I look like a wimp.

"What's wrong?" Violet leans close.

"Just tired."

"Rees." She draws out my name.

Yeah, I'm full of it, and there's no hiding it from her.

"Not now." I tip my head to Bo and his appendage.

"Fine." She turns away from me and scans the cliff walls. "Will we see Machu Picchu, Diego?"

"No. We're close, but you'd have to take a tour or hike up to get there." Diego points off into the distance.

"That's too bad. I've always wanted to explore there." Violet sinks back in the seat so her head rests on the side of the raft and her feet prop up in her seat.

"We'll have to come back then." The words tumble out of my mouth before I can think through what I'm saying.

"Another place to visit?" She smiles, but it doesn't reach her eyes and is so full of hurt I want to punch myself in the face.

I doubt she'll have anything to do with me after the race if I push for an annulment. I hope she'll see that I only want what's best for her, but she might not take it that way. Maybe if we had just stuck to being engaged or if we hadn't broken her one-kiss rule, we could still be friends, but now I'm not so sure.

My breakfast burns up my throat, and I swallow it down. Indecision and guilt taste a lot like refried beans with eggs. I sink low like Violet and close my eyes.

Am I making too much out of this? What Matt said is true. I've seen sport celebrity relationships fail one after another. But would that happen to Violet and me? What if we could be different from all the others? Matt and Sally made it work. Couldn't we?

I peek over at Violet. Her cheeks shine pink from the sun. She needs to put more sunscreen on, or she'll burn. I reach over and rub the back of my fingers over her cheek. She hums, turns her face into my caress, and opens her eyes.

Should I let myself be selfish and snatch the hope

shining behind the hurt in her eyes? Isn't that what my parents trained me to do? Isn't that what I've always done … exactly whatever I wanted? It's why I left home to snowboard. Selfishness is also why I moved to Alaska. Every major decision of my life, including asking Violet to agree to my fake proposal, I did solely for my benefit.

Violet deserves better than that … than me.

I swallow the regret down and pull my fingers away, keeping my voice as neutral as possible. "You need more sunscreen. You're burning."

I look away and cross my arms over my chest, though I can't stop watching her movements out of my peripheral. Her hands jerk as they pull the lotion out of her bag. She doesn't lean back when she's done, just shoves the bottle in her pack and scans ahead. She holds her shoulders rigidly up by her ears, and I close my eyes to the tension I've put there. I guess the world won't have too much of a surprise when our marriage ends. Just another one to add to the statistics.

Chapter Twenty-Five

Placing my foot on the next tiny ledge as we scramble via a ferrata route up the cliff takes all my energy. It's hard to focus, though. I can't shake the feeling that everything between me and Kemp is about to end. I don't know why he's so withdrawn. He's done a bang-up job at not talking past the superficial since we left Guatemala City—was that three, four days ago?

Who cares?

It seems like an eternity.

I glare up at him as he scurries toward the Skylodge pod we are staying in tonight for a mandatory pit stop. Thankfully, it's the first one of several hanging from the mountain. He won't be able to hide any longer. As soon as the cameras stop rolling and we have privacy, I'm pouncing. I don't care if he's tired or not. He's answering my questions.

My hand slips from the rock, and I lean my body against the mountainside to not fall. Sure, I'm hooked up to climbing gear, but I don't want to expend the energy needed to re-scale the cliff. I need all the stamina I can muster to corner my skittish husband.

"You okay?" Kemp hollers.

"Yes," I answer, then add quietly. "You big lug."

"What?" Kemp peers down.

"Nothing." I take another step up and mumble under my breath. "Now you talk, when we're clinging with fingers and toes to a cliffside in the middle of Peru?"

My eye snags on the camera bouncing from my helmet, and I bite the inside of my cheek to keep from grumbling anymore. How could I forget that the world watches everything we do? I'm exhausted, heart-hurt, and I just want to close the doors to the cameras for the night. I peek up at the pod suspended by cables from the cliff two hundred yards above us. Thirty more minutes, and we should be in the clear.

Surely, I can keep my mouth shut for that long, right?

Normally?

Absolutely.

Dragged down by days of extreme racing and emotional turmoil?

Yeah ... I'm not so confident.

I let out a deep breath and lean back against the harness, taking in Peru's Sacred Valley. Dark clouds hug the top of the lush green mountains shooting up from the valley floor. Crops blanket the ground below like Grandma's patchwork quilts she sells at the farmer's market back home.

Wind filled with the clean scent of promising rain

blows against my face, cooling the sweat beading along my hairline and trailing down my back. This altitude is kicking my rear, and ferrataing, if that's even a word, is no joke. I've done plenty of rock climbing, but scrambling up the cliff like a mountain goat is different.

I glance up at our lodging for the night. The glass pod looks like something out of the future stuck to the rocky cliff. The shape reminds me of those things you put your money in at the bank's drive thru. You know, that container that gets sucked up the tube? Only it's big enough to fit four people, gear, and supposedly a bathroom. Thankfully, we've made it before any other teams and will get the pod to ourselves.

Hopefully, the brewing storm will hold off until we make it to the shelter, and put on a show for us. I've always loved weather watching. Rain, lightning, blizzards—you name it, I'm fascinated by it. A glass tube suspended above the Inca Sacred Valley seems like a pretty stunning place to experience a storm in.

Another gust of wind hits, and I stare at the pod strung to the mountainside. Will it toss back and forth in the upheaval, or will it hold stable? I frown at the thought and reach for the next handhold.

That pod is kind of like mine and Kemp's relationship. It may seem strong enough to weather anything the mountain throws at it, but if one cable holding it up snaps or a bolt comes loose from the rock, the entire thing crashes to the valley floor. I'm not sure if the cables and bolts holding me and Kemp together are industrial-grade or something cheap from the Dollar Store.

Before the race, I totally would have claimed we

weren't just industrial, but North Slope, won't break at negative fifty degrees strong.

Now?

I blink away the tears that sting my eyes and shimmy farther up the rocks. Now, I'm not so sure. It kind of seems like we're just a cheap knock-off—fake—exactly what we started the race as.

I push that thought away and pick up my pace. Memory after memory pops up of Kemp's tenderness and love. Memories of me waking up snuggled tight against his chest, though we started the night apart on our own sides. His arms wrapped around me like he'll never let me go. Or ones of his kisses that scorched my soul, branding him to me. There is no way he could fake that.

Not Kemp. I know him, which means something else is up. If I can get to the bottom of it, then I can fix us before our cables snap and tumble us to destruction.

Wow.

That was dramatic, even for me.

Yet, I can't help feeling I'm right.

I finally make it to the wood platform that stretches from the rock wall to the top of the pod where the hatch to climb in is. Kemp sits off on the far side of the platform, gazing out over the valley growing darker each second. His down-turned mouth and shoulders pulled low opposes the Kemp I'm used to, the Kemp that dives into an adventure as fast and freely as I do.

My Kemp's face would shine with the awe this valley deserves. This Kemp doesn't align. It's like I'm staring at someone who's stolen his body.

He glances up at me, and his mouth pulls into a half smile that doesn't reach his eyes. "We made it."

"Yeah. We did." I drink from the water bottle he hands up to me and stare across the valley as a stronger gust hits.

"Come. Let's get you in, and we'll bring you dinner." Our guide motions to the hatch his partner has opened.

I nod, walk across the boards, and climb down the ladder into the glass tube. Two single beds line the walls in the middle section of the pod with a walkway to a large bed stretched across the width on the far end. Beautifully woven pillows decorate the plain bedding, making me yearn to have time to browse through a local market. A small window is propped open like a tiny awning, letting in the smell of the coming storm.

A bathroom is behind me, separated from the rest of the pod by a heavy insulated curtain. It'll be weird and thrilling using it with all the windows facing out. I mean, I'm Alaskan, so doing my business in the wild isn't anything new. However, the view has never been this enthralling before. Kemp's feet appear above me, so I scoot toward the big bed and toss my pack on one of the small ones.

"Get comfortable, and we'll bring dinner over shortly. We'll be in the pod next door. If you need anything, use the walkie-talkie," the guide says before closing the hatch.

"Well, this is nice." Kemp sets his pack next to mine.

"Yep." I take off my helmet and hold it so the camera points at my face. "Well, world, don't know if you're watching, but this is the Reeses signing off. See ya tomorrow for the next adventure."

I smile and wave at the lens before powering the camera down. My expression drops as fast as the helmet where I gently toss it on the bed. I don't know why I said the Reeses instead of just Violet and Kemp. Maybe I'm more passive aggressive than I thought. I close my eyes at that thought. That is not who I want to be.

"Glad we can get a break from the cameras for a while." Kemp sighs and sets his helmet next to mine.

"Yeah, except the drones." I take off my shoes, step onto the stool, and climb onto the edge of the bed.

"Right. Drones." Kemp's neck darkens, and he shoves his hands in his pockets and stares out the glass.

Bo had warned they'd be flying drones up to get footage of us in the pods throughout the night and to keep activities PG-13. Now, my face heats with the memory of his wink. Kemp and I haven't gone past kissing, but who's to say we couldn't? We are married. Maybe sealing the deal, so to speak, would help Kemp with whatever doubt he has?

I clench my fingers into the sage green cotton comforter. No, if Kemp really doesn't want this marriage, doesn't want us, then I can't have memories of us together like that haunting me. Keeping the other precious ones from the race below the surface is going to be hard enough.

Thunder rumbles low up the valley. I peek over my shoulder, amazed at how dark the sky is. Our guides better hustle if they don't want to get drenched.

Another rumble sounds closer and echoes up the valley. A few drops of water ping sporadically against the glass. The wind rattles the window still propped open.

The outside world builds in anticipation, rushing by to help the storm along. But inside the pod, the atmosphere settles thick. Each breath is harder to take. My anxiety bubbles up my throat like those experiments with soda and Mentos. I open my mouth to spew my questions when a knock on the hatch has me swallow them down. I'm choking on them, but no one can know what Kemp and I have done. How we lied, even if the lie turned real—at least for me.

"Dinner." The guide lowers the basket to Kemp, filling the pod with a spicy, rich scent that makes my stomach growl. "Buenas noches."

We mumble our good nights back, but I doubt he heard over the whoosh of the wind. Kemp sets the basket on the bed, turns the lock holding the eating tray up closest to me, then pats the spot on the twin bed behind it.

"Come eat." He pulls out the first covered plate. "Looks like potatoes and some kind of meat." He holds it up to his nose and takes a deep whiff. "Oh man, this smells amazing. There's also salad and dessert."

I slide off the bed and sit behind the tray. When he sets a glass of water on the wood, I gulp half of it down. My mouth and throat are so dry, I'm not sure if I'll be able to get words out or food down.

The part of me that wants to stay in the safety bubble and push everything negative down doesn't want to talk about what's really going on. I stare out the window where the sun's descent adds a dark magenta to the thunderclouds. Keeping to the surface like Kemp is doing would be so much easier.

Isn't that my M.O. too?

I mean, it's why I made that stupid one-kiss rule to begin with, to keep the potential for hurtful or bad memories to a minimum. If life only ever stays light and fun, then I don't have to work so hard. Those types of memories are easy to keep down deep and don't ache when they manage to break through to the top.

"What do you want?" Kemp's question snaps my stare from the storm.

"What?" The sharp pain right at the top of my throat cuts my question off.

Is he finally opening up?

"What do you want?" Kemp points to the food.

A tear breaks free, and I turn back to the glass so he doesn't see. Why won't he talk to me? I close my eyes, giving my head a small shake. Why is he holding so much from me? Not trusting me?

Can you blame him?

No, not really. I mean, I kept my H-SAM from him. Didn't trust him with all of me, so why would he confide in me?

"Violet?" Kemp's hand on my shoulder breaks the last of my strength.

"I want to know what's going on." A sob garbles the last bit, but I turn and lean my back against the glass. "I want to know why you can hardly look at me now."

"Wilde, I—" He rubs his hand across his neck, his shoulders drooping.

He clenches his teeth so hard that his cheek muscles pop. What could I have done to make him like this? A shiver rushes through me, and I pull my knees up to my chest.

"Please, just tell me what I did so I can make this better, make us better." I hate the pleading in my voice, but I'm desperate.

"You didn't do anything. This is all me."

I snort. Isn't that the typical break-up line?

"No, really." He slumps on the opposite bed. "I

shouldn't have ever suggested we do this. Definitely shouldn't have agreed to the wedding."

His regret punches me in the stomach. I pull my knees tighter to me. So, everything *was* a lie? How could I have been so wrong about him?

"Wait, baby—Violet, that came out all wrong." Kemp rubs his fingers over his eyes. "Can I make this any worse?" He fists his fingers and looks up. Tears brighten his eyes. "I have been so selfish. Guess that's not surprising. It's in my blood."

"No—"

"Yes, Violet, I am." He breathes a humorless laugh. "My parents trained me well. Made sure I was really good at taking care of numero uno. Every single decision I've ever made has been for myself. Every single one."

I shake my head as memory after memory rushes in of him during search and rescue, helping Sawyer, and donating to people around town.

"It's true. Leaving my parents, moving to Alaska, proposing to you were all to make life for me better."

"That doesn't mean you're selfish."

"Doesn't it though? My lifestyle—homes in two places, traveling to competitions, constantly having my life under a microscope—that life isn't good for a family. Think about it. Do you really want to be away from your parents, your sister, and cousins for most of the year?"

"It'll be hard but being with you will be worth it."

"Living out of a suitcase isn't fun. It's exhausting."

"You forget I love to travel."

"What about when we have kids? Dragging them around the world just to watch me play in the snow isn't the way a family is supposed to be raised. It's not healthy."

"Who says?" Now, I'm mad. He's made all these assumptions about what would be good for me, for our hypothetical kids, based on what? I scoot to the edge of the bed.

"Just look at the divorce rate of professional athletes." He throws his arms wide like the stats are written on the glass.

"We aren't like other people." I stand and poke him in the chest.

He brushes my finger away. "I don't want that life for you."

"You don't get to decide that."

"Vi, we started this guise of a relationship knowing it'd end." He crosses his arms over his chest and swallows. "I ... I say we keep to the original plan."

I stumble backwards and come up against the big bed. My vision blurs as my entire face stings from the hurtful words. He can't mean this. Not really.

"Yeah, well, then you shouldn't have shown me how much you love me, because I love you just as much, and I can't give up on us that easily."

"I didn't—"

I tap my head as a tear breaks free. "Perfect memory, remember? Any lie you say now, I won't believe, because I can see your actions over and over and over in my head."

"Violet, I can't let you have a life you'll hate. It's not fair." He pulls on his hair, making it stick out in all directions. He sniffs and rubs the back of his hand across his face.

"What's not fair is you thinking you get to make that

decision." I step onto the stool and scoot backward across the bed. "I'm not hungry."

I climb under the covers fully dressed and pull the sheet over my head. Lightning strikes outside, followed by a bang of thunder that unleashes the downpour promised. At least with the noise of the storm, Kemp won't hear me crying.

Chapter Twenty-Six

-*KEMP*-

You know, I never figured I'd be at a South American icon of ski resorts at the height of the snow season and be completely miserable. I scan the rocky terrain above me, then the treeless slopes below. I've thought about coming down here to Portillo, Chile for years. Have a whole "Board South America" game plan in my Notes app. So, I should be living this moment up, but because I've hurt the only person who has really known and loved me more than can ever be forgiven, I can't even enjoy the experience.

Yesterday, after zip lining from the Skypod, we flew from Cusco, Peru to Santiago, Chile. From there, we hopped on a shuttle to the legendary bright yellow Hotel Portillo on the shore of the Lake of the Inca.

Could we get right on with the challenge?

Nope.

Of course, it'll take most of the day to hike the mountain to the off-limits ski run, which meant I had to endure another heart-wrenching night with the wife I want to keep but shouldn't. So, when Matt and Sally showed up at the dining room when we were finishing dinner, I snagged on the opportunity to not have to face Violet alone in the hotel room.

Big mistake. Staying in the lobby, chatting with the couple, should have been the perfect distraction, but Violet took the opportunity to ask Sally questions about the struggles of being married to an athlete. Despite Matt's subtle shaking of his head at his wife's answers, they gave me hope that maybe a life with Violet could work. But is that hope still tainted with selfishness?

"So …" Matt huffs out quick breaths behind me. "A lot of what my wife said last night was true. You know, about being married in the spotlight."

"What about your whole 'marriage is ten times harder' bit?" I glance up to see how much farther we have left to get to the top of the mountain.

"Yeah … that may have been the hike through volcanic hell talking."

"Dude!" I stop and look over my shoulder at him. "I've been stressing about putting Violet through all that."

"Sorry, man." He shrugs and scrunches his face. "I mean, it is harder, but with the right person, it's doable. More than doable."

I jerk back to the goat trail and huff up the path. Violet totally is a person who could rise above the pettiness the limelight brings. Am I?

I scramble up the rest of the mountain, jab my skis into the bank, and plop on the snow. Too bad they wouldn't let me use a snowboard to get down this off-limits run. I mean, I'm good on skis. I was actually on a ski team and everything until I turned fourteen and probably could have gone to the Olympics. According to my parents, skis are more sophisticated than a board. So, you can imagine how pleased they were when I rebelled.

This run, with its steep descent through a couloir in the rocks opening to a slope that doesn't level out until nearly the bottom, would be gnarly on a snowboard. It's going to be sick on skis too. No wonder the network had the forty-page questionnaire about what skills we had. (Okay, forty is an exaggeration, but it was long.) I just hope no one stretched the truth, because this run's sheer drop, while straight once through the rock gap, could do some serious harm to someone who's only been on greens and blues.

"For what it's worth"—Matt drops in the snow next to me, his chest heaving from the climb—"I think you and Violet have what it takes to beat the statistic."

"Why's that?"

Is the dude just stroking my ego or something to make himself not look so bad? He hardly knows me or Violet.

"I've been around a lot of couples in the racing world. We like to all pretend we're friends off the track, you know, even though we'd rather ram their tailgate on the way home." Matt chuckles. "Remember that Tom Cruise movie *Days of Thunder* where Cruise's character and Rowdy are racing in the city streets but are cool and calm in front of the cameras?"

"Yeah." I vaguely remember watching that movie at a friend's house once.

"Well, that's about how it goes. You have a few core people you can trust, and the rest are out to knock you down." Matt sits forward and leans his forearms on his knees. "Anyway, I've watched how you and Violet interact. Even though it's obvious you've been in a funk with her, and, again, sorry. That's probably my fault. But even with that, she's still sinking her teeth in, unwilling to just let go. And you—"

Matt blows a short laugh out and shakes his head.

"I what?"

"Man, you look at her as if she's the sun, the moon, *and* all the stars in the sky."

"No, I don't."

Matt chuckles again, and my neck heats up.

"When you think no one is looking, you totally do. It's not a bad thing, especially with the friendship you two have. That's how your relationship started, right?" He raises an eyebrow at me.

"Yeah. She's the best friend I ever had. She's kept me grounded the last three years since I moved up to Alaska and my career exploded."

He nods like my confession wasn't a surprise. "That's another reason you two will make it. You built your marriage on something more than just attraction, lust, and fame. Don't get me wrong. I know couples who met in the spotlight and are killing it. It's just so much easier when there's a base of friendship to touch down on when the highs of being a celebrity pop." He claps me on the shoulder and jerks his chin toward the people milling at the run's start. "Should we get to it?"

"Sure."

Staring across the mountain ridges, I sit a moment longer as Matt stands. The churning that's gnawed my stomach since Guatemala City eases to a low burn. Maybe Matt is right. I want to believe him, to snatch on to what he said and hold it close. My gaze trails to the bottom of the valley where Violet waits at the bright yellow resort. It's like a beacon down there, shining my way home. Only one question remains. Do I let it draw me in?

Chapter Twenty-Seven

-Violet-

Just so you know, waiting is torture. It's been hours since Kemp and Matt left to make the trek up the mountain. Long minutes of watching their progress on foot from the ski lift's end up the rocky trail. Kemp kept his lead the entire way, though if I hadn't seen him get on the lift first or noticed the red stripe on the back of his helmet, it'd be hard to distinguish the two men apart with the matching winter gear the resort provided.

He'd been on the top of the mountain for eight minutes and—I glance at my watch—thirty-nine seconds. How long is he going to rest? I pace along the rocky ridge the race officials brought Sally and me to when the men got close to the top. Its vantage point overlooks the Super-C Kemp will jet down. I peek at my watch again, frustrated that it's only been twenty-one seconds since the last time I looked.

I stop, take a deep breath, and relax my hands. Well, try to relax. That hike up Roca Jack couldn't have been easy. Just because I've spent the last few hours lounging on the resort porch, sipping hot chocolate or having snowball fights with the kids hanging around the cameras, doesn't mean Kemp has to snap to it. I close my eyes and pray for peace and safety. While I'm here, I might as well list all my concerns. It's much more useful than fretting.

"Look. Kemp's lining up," Sally gushes and hands me the binoculars.

My eyes whip open, and I snatch the glasses from her hands so fast she jumps back a little. "Sorry."

"Oh, honey. I know exactly how you feel. I'm so nervous for Matt I might ruin the pretty white snow by upchucking my hot chocolate all over it." She places her mittened fingers on her cheeks. "At least Kemp's used to the snow. We ski and all, but nothing like this."

Her voice trembles at the end, and I wrap my arm around her and pull her into a side hug. She shakes like a leaf against me. Here I am, mentally urging Kemp to hurry it up—I mean, this is what he does for a living, granted usually on a board instead of two sticks, but still, he's totally got this—and Sally's worked herself into a tizzy.

"Hey. Don't worry. See how the mountain forms that C through the rocks?" I point up where the run starts.

"Uh huh." Sally's hesitant voice barely reaches past her lips.

"Well, the snow will just keep them in the funnel, and the rest of the run past the rocks is smooth as butter." I give her a squeeze.

Technically, it's the truth. I've snowboarded down mountaintops like this back in Alaska with Kemp. Granted, the couloirs have never been this long or narrow, but if Matt just stays in the middle and keeps tight, he'll make it. Hopefully, he can watch how Kemp does it and follow suit.

"Oh, look. The flag is waving." Sally points to the top of the hill where a big red flag is bouncing back and forth on the edge of the cliff.

I slam the binoculars up so fast they knock against my face. "Shoot."

Rubbing my forehead to make the tears disappear, I place the glasses up more gently. Kemp rocks twice on the ledge but doesn't go. Why is he hesitating? That's not like him at all. Nerves skitter up my arms and tingle through my fingers. If he's hesitating, then the slope must be worse than it looks from down here. I stare through the binoculars, my stomach twisting tighter and tighter with each second he stalls.

Finally, he leans back on his skis and pushes off with his poles. The crowds gathered on the rock ridges on the other side of the run shout cheers. A trail of sparks from a firework shoots up toward the mountain from the people and explodes into a sparkle of lights with a bang that echoes up the valley.

I lower the binoculars as Kemp makes the curve, my gaze snagging on movement on the mountain. The snow sloughs off the rocks in a line that slides lower and lower. My heart flies into my throat.

Avalanche.

"No." I tear my gaze from the rolling snow and focus on Kemp. "No, no, no."

The snow builds into a billowing cloud of white just as Kemp shoots from the stone gap. The raging beast tumbles behind his skis, making his body jerk as he compensates for the crashing snow. He'll never make it.

Memories of my sister, Sadie, buried in an avalanche

rush from the depths of my brain, forcing their way before me. I push them aside. They can't bombard me now, not when I need to keep all my focus on Kemp. If I can see exactly where the avalanche overtakes him, I can better pinpoint where to look for him. Every second counts when someone is buried beneath pounds of snow that pack like cement around them.

That thought forces up the replay of finding Sadie and her best friend, Melinda, the memory as real as if I'm there again.

Fear chills me at the sight of the cabin crushed into a tumbled tomb of logs by the force of the snow. I rush into the cabin behind my mom, screaming at the sight of Melinda's eleven-year-old body in a case of white. Her eyes stare blankly into space. Sadie is unconscious on the opposite side, her lips blue with hypothermia. The snow had pushed her into the wood stove, burning through her sweatshirt and melting the skin on her arms and collarbone practically off. The smell of burnt flesh saturates the small opening the tumbled cabin had created.

"Stop." I shake my head to dislodge the playback as bile rushes up my throat.

My focus must be on the now. Every cell of my body freezes as the snow rushes over the back of Kemp's skis and bucks him off balance. I note the location against the rocks on the opposite side, then scan the rolling rush of white for any glimpse of the bright yellow Portillo Ski coat. I don't remember them putting on beacons, so, unless they had him put it on at the top, there won't be any pinpointing his location.

There. An arm and shoulder peek from the white farther down the slope a second before the snow boils back over. One ski shoots from the rolling snow, while the other pokes up and tumbles back under. Then, out of the churning, bright hunter-orange flashes. Relief almost makes my knees buckle. He's wearing an avalanche airbag. Praise God.

I keep my eyes on it. Even with the safety backpack, he can still get buried or sustain life-threatening injuries. Could still die.

Melinda's shocked expression stares at me.

I blink, clearing my vision of her to the slope before me. If I had gone with Dad and Sadie the night before instead of coming up with Mom the next day, the snow would've buried me too.

The rolling slows to a stop, and I sprint across the packed snow. A swath of orange peeks from the white. Others make it there before me, but I push them aside to get to Kemp.

"Excuse us." Sally's sharp voice hollers right behind me. "Move out of the way!"

The circle opens, and I stumble at the amount of snow covering Kemp. Three men lift chunks of white from around the orange. Kemp's boot with the ski still attached sticks out awkwardly at an angle that can only mean a major break. How much of the rest of him is busted up?

Sally grabs my hand and wraps her other arm around mine in a hug. I want to push the men aside and dig like a wild woman, but I can see from their meticulous yet quick motions that they know what they are doing. They finally get Kemp's head free from the snow and pull off his helmet, but it's not Kemp.

"No, Matt!" Sally screams beside me, and I wrap my arms around her to keep her from rushing forward.

A sob rips from me as I scan the mountaintop for a sign of Kemp. How is it Matt buried in the snow? Kemp had arrived at the top first. I'm sure of it. Why didn't he go first?

"He's alive!" one man digging Matt out yells, and Sally falls to her knees.

I go down with her, too weak to stay standing. Besides, she needs someone to hold her together. With the relief, the memories cascade as if what little will I had to keep them at bay breaks. They're flooding me with warring images, sounds, and smells from the past. Finding Sadie unmoving and buried in the snow. The months of healing she went through for her burns. Other rescue missions I've gone on. All of that mixed with what just happened in a painful rush.

"We've got a helicopter on standby to take him to the hospital." Ivy steps up beside us. I haven't talked to her since Vegas. "Sally, as soon as he's out of the snow, you two will fly out, okay?"

Sally nods, her sobs coming so hard I doubt she can speak.

"I have another helicopter that will bring Kemp off of the mountain as soon as Matt is gone." Ivy presses her lips together like she needs to in order to stop talking.

She had everything so planned out. Did she not have a contingency in place for this kind of emergency?

"Okay," I answer through the bombardment in my brain.

Ten minutes later, Sally climbs into the helicopter with Matt. He broke his femur, probably more bones than that, but with the quick work of the diggers, they should get him to the hospital to catch anything life threatening. I stumble off toward the resort.

The memories reel so quickly now that I may never

get them back under control. My head will rip open at any moment from the pain and assault. Finding my way to the resort, I make it into the elevator. I'm shaking so badly my knees buckle with the whoosh of the elevator moving. My arms lock against the railing mounted to the wall to stay standing.

I stare at my reflection in the mirrored door, but I don't see myself. All I see is Melinda and Sadie and all the others. The doors slide open, and I tumble out, rushing to the trashcan in the hall and losing my hot chocolate.

Somehow, I make it to our room. My hand trembles hard, and it takes four tries to get the keycard in the lock and the door open. I strip out of my jacket and head to the bathroom. Maybe if I can just warm up, I can get the flood to slow enough to push the nightmares back to the depths where I want them.

I turn on the shower and take off my jeans. Tripping as my foot sticks in the bottom, I finally get out of them and stagger into the shower without taking anything else off. I just want the warmth.

Just want to forget.

The hot flow hits, and I flinch at the burning heat. It doesn't help the rapid playback of life's worst memories from streaming. I lean my head against the tile, sliding down the wall until I curl into a tight ball. My sobs ache against my ribs.

"Stop." I squeeze my eyes shut tight to the memories, though I know that won't help either. "Please … please stop."

It's useless. They'll never stop.

Chapter Twenty-Eight

-*Kemp*-

The instant the helicopter touches down, I dash toward the resort. Waiting up at the top of the mountain took every ounce of my patience. I could have easily skied down the chute once the avalanche finished, but—noooo—safety and all that. Sure, the race officials received updates, but I needed to be down there.

Needed to make sure Violet was okay.

"Kemp!" Ivy hollers, holding up her hand for me to stop.

I don't hold back the groan of frustration.

"I know. I'll make it quick," Ivy clips in an efficient tone. "The resort has their experts checking the snow's stability, and we should be able to continue with the race tomorrow."

"Fine." I try to push past, but she stops me.

I raise my eyebrow at her.

"Tomorrow morning at sunup, if we get the go ahead, a helicopter will take you to the top for your run.

You already hiked Roca Jack once. I'm not going to make you do it again." She smiles at me like she's given me a prize.

"Ivy, don't take this wrong, but I couldn't care less what you make me do. Want me to walk naked through a snowstorm while juggling pineapples? Fine, show me the way … tomorrow. Right now, all I care about is finding my wife."

"She's in your room." Ivy tips her head, her mouth twitching up on one side.

I sprint for the elevators. When they move too slowly, I take off for the stairs. This intense necessity to see her —to hold her—overwhelms me so much it's scary. Yet, I can't ignore it anymore.

When I make it to the room, I slam the keycard in the slot so hard it bends. The green light blinks, and I turn the knob. If I go barreling in there, I'll freak Violet out. I take two deep breaths to calm down, then push the door open.

Panic wells back up when I take in the empty room. I turn to go search the resort when the shower running in the bathroom registers. Tapping on the door, I lean my head against the doorjamb and close my eyes to the relief loosening my muscles. When she doesn't answer, I knock louder.

Nothing.

I press my ear to the door. Her mumbling faintly reaches me over the noise of the shower. She still hasn't answered me. I pace away from the door, pushing my hand through my hair.

I can't go in. We haven't gotten to that point in our relationship, especially with my jerkface attitude the last few days. Staring blankly out the window, I struggle with what to do. I still worry that I'm only wanting the relationship because of selfishness, but I also know we work. I need her to be whole, and from what she said in the Skypod, she's not willing to let go of me either. Huffing out a sigh, I walk back up to the barrier between me and my wife.

My wife.

If she'll still have me. I'll show her how much I love her, make up my boneheadedness to her somehow. First, though, I have to see if she's okay.

"Please … stop." Violet's anguished plea muffles through the door, and my hesitance is gone.

"Violet, baby, you okay?" I knock on the door, but she still doesn't answer me.

All right. I'll just open it a crack and peek in. Maybe she can't hear me over the water. If everything is fine, I'll wait out here for her to finish. With a sweat-slicked hand, I turn the knob.

"Violet?"

Thick steam punches me in the face, instantly making me hot. I glance toward the shower, keeping my gaze high where her head should be and not lower. I don't want to be even more in the doghouse than I already am. The water's running, but she's not there.

Opening the door farther, my stomach hardens and drops like a boulder kicked off the top of Roca Jack. She's bunched in the bottom of the shower in her soaked North STAR Kennel T-shirt, bright pink underwear, and moose-wearing-stocking-caps socks. Her legs curl up against her chest, her head tucked into her knees as she rocks back and forth. Water splashes over her head and runs down her face, but I don't think she notices.

"Baby?" My word garbles in my throat, choking me.

She's never, not once in all the rough search-and-rescue missions we've been on, looked like this. I yank my coat down and kick my boots off. When I open the glass shower door, more steam rolls over me. The scorching water hurts as it pelts my arm and shoulders. I turn the knob to cool down the water so it doesn't boil our skin off and squat down next to Violet.

"Vi." I touch her shoulder, and she flinches, curling in on herself even more. "Vi, baby, it's me."

I push my hand along her shoulder and move her wet hair off her cheek. When she finally lifts her head, her puffy face and red eyes break my heart. Her chin trembles, and she reaches a shaking hand toward me.

"Kemp?" Her voice breaks, and I lose it.

I don't even hide the tears that pool and splash down my cheeks.

"I'm here. We're okay." I take her hand in mine.

"No. I'm not okay." Her frantic grasp rips me apart even more. "I'll never be okay."

"Shh, that's not true." I sit next to her and wrap my arm around her.

"They won't stop." She pushes her hand to her head and leans it against my chest.

"What won't?"

"The memories. They've broken the surface, and I can't get them back down. They won't stop playing. Sadie and Melinda stuck in the snow. The smell, Kemp. I can smell Sadie's burned skin. Then there's the avalanche overtaking you … I mean, Matt." A sob shakes her body as her words tumble out faster and faster. "I'm living them over and over again. I can't … I can't get them back below the surface. They're drowning me."

I hadn't considered that she couldn't keep the memories at bay. She explained how she's learned to control them and float above them, keeping her eyes focused on the now. She said her one-kiss rule kept things easier. Did she mean keep the possibility of hurtful events like break-ups and heartaches from haunting her like these memories are? I never imagined the depth of what this superpower did and how it could harm her. How could I even combat an enemy that's in her mind?

"I remember the first day I met you." I'm not sure where the thought came from, but I'm rolling with it. "I'd just signed up with Search and Rescue, and your dad made me go on a rappelling training day."

She lifts her head, her voice weak and trembling. "I remember."

"All the volunteers met on the top of the cliff with your uncle, and your dad was at the bottom, hollering up commands. You came over right away when I pulled up and threaded your arm through mine like you were greeting a friend you'd known forever. It wasn't at all fake. I remember thinking I'd never met someone as open and welcoming as you. Your hair was a soft pink all over then, like the color of the sky when the sun starts to set over the ocean."

"You had on that ridiculous shirt with a halibut on the front that said 'Bite Me' on it." She's looking at me, her eyes staring at my face, but not really seeing me.

"Yeah, yeah I did." I laugh slightly, running my thumb over her fingers to try and relax them. "Your uncle had two ropes thrown over the edge, and me, wanting to establish that I knew what the heck I was doing and deserved to be there, volunteered to go first. I mean, it was a basic rappel backwards over the edge. No big deal. I was bouncing my way down the cliff about ten feet from the top when your dad hollered for you to stop. The sight of you coming over that cliff face first on that other rope is something I'll never forget. Man, you were so beautiful with your thrilled smile on your face and the wink you threw me when you sped past. Here I was, thinking I'd show off a bit, and you blow us all out of the water with your stunt."

"Dad was furious. Lectured me about taking training seriously and not showboating."

I run the back of my fingers over her cheek. "I think I fell in love with you that day."

"What?" That snaps her attention to me and not the past.

"Yeah. I didn't really understand at the time, but I'm certain that's what happened. It wasn't just your risk-taking or your wild beauty, either."

"No?"

"No. It was so much more than that. You pulled me into your circle without a second guess or ulterior motive. I never felt awkward with you, not once. Then your dad invited me to their place for a barbecue, and I was suddenly enveloped into a family like I'd never seen before. I didn't want it to end, so I determined I'd do whatever it took to not screw up what I'd found. I'd be the best friend you could ask for, the stray your family would adopt in, and I'd finally have the family I always longed for but never knew just how much I needed." I rub my thumb along her jawline and huff a laugh. "That probably doesn't make any sense at all."

"It does." She leans her cheek against my hand, a crease forming along her forehead like she's in pain.

"Tell me about when Sawyer was born." I shift and pull her onto my lap so she's facing me. "I want all the details."

Maybe if I can get her to focus on wonderful memories of her favorite person in the entire world, she can get control of the bad ones. A smile lifts the corner of her lips. Her face relaxes as she tells me about seeing Sawyer for the first time in the hospital. She leans against my palms spread across her back, her hands dancing through the air as she talks about the way the light filtered through the vertical blinds and how Sawyer's mouth puckered as he rooted for food.

With a sigh, she sets her hands on my shoulders and stares into my eyes. "Thank you. It's difficult to function when the hard memories bombard me. Even now, they want to force my attention on them."

"I will always be here to remind you of the good, Violet."

"Always?" Her fingers trail up my shoulders and skim my neck.

"As long as you want me." I spread my hand across her back, tempted to pull her against me, but, because I've been an idiot and pushed her away, she has to make the first move.

"Forever." She breathes and leans her forehead on to mine. "I want you forever, Kemp Rees. I never want to let go."

She captures my cheeks in her small palms and kisses

me with such hope and abandon that I could soar to the top of Roca Jack without a helicopter. I fist her wet shirt in my hands and pull her flush to me. This is love and happiness. This is belonging to something bigger than myself.

I wrap her hair through my fingers, pull her head to the side, and trail my lips up over her soft skin. The last days of pushing her away have left me starving for her, like life had been sucked out of my very cells without her. She runs her hands down my chest and untucks my shirt. Her light touch along the skin on my back rushes heat through my muscles and into my veins, scorching my body from my head to my toes.

I should have turned the faucet all the way to cold.

"Kemp." She breathes my name against my mouth, kissing me before I can answer.

Not that I could manage forming actual words at the moment. She bites my bottom lip and pulls away a fraction of a millimeter. It's too far, but before I can complain, she talks again.

"Let's make new memories. Um … married memories." The slight tremble of her fingers against my back and pause in her voice can't hide her uncertainty.

I want to obliterate all the doubts I've put in her mind. It's not possible with the way her brain traps every moment for automatic recall. Yet, from this minute forward, for the rest of my life, I'm determined she'll never question my love for her again. I'm not naïve enough to think life will be sunshine and roses, but I'll do whatever I can so she always trusts the bond we have.

"I love you, Violet." I skim my hand along the hem of her shirt. "Let's fill that incredible brain of yours with so many bright and euphoric moments that the others have no room to surface."

Her smile bursts upon her face, happy tears spilling over to mix with the shower water. How can I be so blessed to have her in my life? She may have the ability to remember every moment's details, but this is one image that I'll cherish until I die —possibly longer.

Chapter Twenty-Nine

-Violet-

As we paddle our small kayak across the water toward a boat anchored close to Iguazú Falls, I tip my head up and take in what the Argentinian jungle offers. The largest waterfall in the world thunders before us. A toucan soars above us. Sunlight filters through the light cloud cover and dances on the water's surface.

I've never felt as content as I do right now.

I shouldn't.

We saw both the basketball and Marshpillow teams in the jungle while we searched for birds—a green-billed toucan, green-winged saltator, magpie tanager, and my favorite, the fluffy blue manakin with a bright red cap of feathers on its head, among a handful of others. We found the birds first, yet the other teams arrived at the Gauraní village while we finished learning a traditional dance from the local children.

"Hey, slacker. Paddle. The basketball boys are in the water." Kemp squeezes me with his legs stretched out on both sides of me.

I will say one thing, I like this simple style of kayak. It's more cozy than the ones we have at home with separate seats. I scooch back so I'm cradled against him.

"Violet."

"Can't I kiss my husband?" I lean sideways just enough to peek up at him over my shoulder.

Never taking his eyes off mine, he sets his paddle in the boat, cups my cheek with his palm like I'm fragile as glass (and, oh, how I really like it when he does that), then, with such slowness it's torture, he lowers his mouth to mine.

His kiss brushes softly against my lips, and I sigh in resignation. We have a checkpoint to get to and opponents skimming toward us. This isn't the time to be smooching.

Just when I'm about to pull away, he pushes his hand deep into my hair, sending all the strands to stand up straight by their roots, and kisses me with such passion my entire body is about to combust. I'm so, so glad I had that silly one-kiss rule. I want all my memories of these kinds of soul-moving, firework-exploding kisses to be with Kemp and only him. When he pulls back, we're both sucking air and a little dazed. I might need to roll off the kayak and take a dip to cool off.

"Wow." I sigh.

"Yeah." He presses another quick kiss to my lips. "Ready to paddle now?"

"Right. Race. Million bucks each."

I move back to my spot and dig my paddle into the water. I turn to check the others' progress.

Tyrone whistles from behind us, and Michael yells, "Get a room!"

My cheeks and ears heat for an entirely different

reason. Oh, goodness. With Kemp around, I keep forgetting the entire world is watching. Okay, maybe not the entire world, but definitely my mom and dad.

I cringe at the camera mounted on the front of the kayak. "Sorry, Dad."

Kemp chuckles behind me. "I'm not."

I swat his leg and paddle faster. Jill waits on the deck, so this is definitely a checkpoint. My excitement for what's next bubbles in my chest.

"Where do you think we're going now? Paraguay? Bolivia? Maybe we'll circle back north and go to Venezuela or Colombia?"

"As long as you're with me, I'm game." Kemp squeezes his legs around me in a hug.

If there weren't a dozen cameras pointing in our direction, I'd crawl back to him and show my husband just how happy he makes me. Since we already gave the people a smoochfest, and the other team is closing in, my show of appreciation will have to wait until we find some privacy. I bite my bottom lip as memories of our last private moment replay. Okay, yeah … we definitely need to paddle faster.

The kayak bumps against the side of the boat, and I scramble onto the deck. Kemp boards right beside me as the thump of the other team's kayak alerts their arrival. Dang. They're fast.

I grab Kemp's hand and rush down the walkway between the helm and the railing on the starboard side. I peek through the window of the cabin and stumble on my own feet. Just as I'm about to hit the deck, Kemp scoops me up and throws me over his shoulder. This isn't the most flattering way to get to the checkpoint, and I almost tell Kemp to put me down. Tyrone rounds the corner on the opposite side of the boat right after we do. I throw all dignity out the window and pound on Kemp's back.

"Go, go, go!" I'm half laughing, half shouting as all the blood rushes to my head.

Kemp slides me to the checkpoint mat a second before Tyrone barrels onto it. I almost fall again getting out of the lug's way, so Kemp pulls me into a hug with my back pressed against his chest. Michael stumbles up next to Tyrone, placing his hands on his knees.

"Phew, that was close." Kemp's exhale blows against my hair, and I nod.

"You couldn't run any faster? We almost had them." Tyrone pushes on Michael's shoulder.

"Dude, these two are crazy fast." Michael shakes his head. "Besides, if you had listened to me about the green-winged saltator, we would have beaten them easy."

"Whatever." Tyrone waves his hand, and I chuckle.

I'm glad we've gotten to know them the little that we have. Their constant ribbing reminds me of my family back home.

Jill clears her throat, and we all turn to her. She has that congratulatory smile on her face that she's had at each checkpoint. She really has been a wonderful host for the show. I wonder what her expression is for those at the end of the line.

"Well, that was the closest check-in we've had yet. You all definitely know how to put on a show." Her sparkling gaze bounces between us, then settles on me and Kemp. "Kemp, Violet, congratulations. You two are the first to arrive at the Iguazú Falls checkpoint and the winners of the Nature Channel's Race Across the Americas." Her mouth widens to a genuine open mouth smile as her words register.

"What?" My knees give out, and Kemp's arms tighten around me.

"We won?" Kemp's leaning on me like his legs might be jello too.

"Yep. You won." Jill opens her arms wide. "The two of you make an incredible team. You ran an amazing race, one you should be very proud of."

I twist around and throw myself at Kemp. He catches me, lifting me off the ground and spinning in a circle. When he stops and doesn't let me down, I wrap my legs and arms tight around him. I don't care that the world and my dad watch. I'm kissing my husband, and I'm not stopping at one.

Chapter Thirty

I squeeze Violet's hand as the plane bumps onto the airstrip back home in Seward. Nerves bubble in my gut like I chugged a liter of soda. I shouldn't be worried. Violet talked to her parents after we won, and she said they were fine.

I'm not convinced.

Saying things are fine and the situation actually *being* fine are two totally different things. She wasn't on speaker, so I don't know if it was her tenderhearted mom doing all the talking or if both her parents are happy for us.

I catch sight of a small crowd of friends and family waiting for us to land through the tiny airplane window. Will Wilde stands in the front of the pack with his arms crossed and a scowl on his face. I gulp, my hand slicking in cold sweat.

"You sure you don't want to bribe the pilot to just take off without opening the door?" I turn to Violet.

"We could go travel the US like we said, maybe spend a few weeks exploring Moab."

Violet leans over me and peers out the window. "Oh, dear."

"I don't think it'd even take that much money." I squeeze her fingers tighter, not even a little ashamed my fear is showing.

Her dad is scary, especially when it comes to "his girls."

"Don't worry." She pats my arm with her free hand like her little love tap will ease all my worries. "Even if he's upset, what can he really do to us?"

"Um … I can think of about a million things, and none of them are pretty."

"Baby." The way she rolls her eyes makes it clear that wasn't an endearment.

"Na-uh." I counter, then quickly add when her eyebrow rises. "Okay, maybe a little." It hitches up more. "A big baby. All right?"

She smiles, leans over, and brushes her lips to mine. "Dad loves you. He just might be a little upset about the whole elopement thing and us having to be gone once the snowboarding season starts. When he sees how in love we are and that it's not fake, he'll get over it."

While we didn't get all of our future figured out, we know that, at least for now, I'll keep on the snowboarding circuit, and she'll come with me. If she had said she couldn't leave Alaska, I would've quit. Nothing is worth losing her over.

We still need to talk to Denali, Sadie, and Rory about the kennel, but Violet even has a plan for that. She wants to use part of her funds from the reality show with Drew to hire her cousin. Violet will still work when we're here, but hiring someone else will make sure the others don't have to take on her responsibilities and the kennel doesn't suffer. It might not work long-term, but it'll do until the kennel can afford the employee on its own.

The pilot lowers the ramp to disembark, and the time of reckoning has arrived. I lead Violet to her family—our family—holding Will's gaze and trying not to crunch Violet's hand with my grip. When we get close, the cheering stops, and I swallow down my nerves.

"Sir, I know we went around getting married backwards, but I want you to know that I'm going to do my best to make Violet happy and feel loved every day of her life." I turn my eyes to her, soaking in the proud smile stretched across her beautiful face. "The thing is she's the world to me, the reason I'm a better man, and my best friend. I'm wild about Violet, and I'd say yes all over again if I had the choice."

She blinks, her eyes sparkling with unshed tears.

"That's good, son." Will steps forward and claps his beefy hand on my shoulder. "Because we're wild about you too."

He pulls me into a hug. I wish I could tell you that I didn't tear up, but I never felt acceptance like I do with the Wildes. I may have escaped to Alaska to find peace, but I never imagined I'd find family.

Epilogue

-Rory-

I watch as Violet and Kemp flit from one person to the next at the celebratory picnic. Uncle Will's manning the smoker filled with moose steaks and fresh salmon. Violet and Kemp move to where Bjorn, Sadie, Denali, and Drew are setting up the croquet set. I take a deep breath, hold it for a handful of seconds, then let the discontent that simmers low in my gut out.

My forehead scrunches, and I shake my head at that thought. Maybe discontent is too strong of a word. I'm happy. The kennel is flourishing, my books are selling well, and I have life well-oiled and maintained.

Ugh. Geez. When did I start thinking about life like a machine I had to sustain?

I roll my shoulders, sore from my morning workout at the gym, hoping to shrug off the humdrums as well. I really shouldn't be over here, sulking. Life is good, comfortable. There is no reason for me to be so gloomy.

Except you're stuck on your plot, the story ideas have dried up, and you can't find your way out.

"Shh. I didn't ask you," I mumble to that inner critic constantly nagging at me lately. "I can fix the story, no problem. Even though I have the love interests dangling over a raging river with no apparent way free, I've got this. Somehow."

"You okay?" Mark walks up with two plates full of food.

"Yep. Just talking to myself." I laugh and grab the plate he extends to me.

He sits beside me, and I catch my mom and aunt nudging each other and smiling at us. Those two. I shake my head. They figure, with the other girls happily in love, it's my time to shine. Little do they know that while I may write award-winning romance novels, I have no firsthand experience with the notion.

Maybe that's the problem with my writing *and* my life? All my insights are from other people's adventures and ordeals. I've been more than happy to live vicariously through those around me and beloved characters I meet in books. Always have been. I push at my potato salad on the plate and try not to dig too deep into that thought.

The gate swings open, and Dax Payton saunters in. My sore muscles stiffen and my fork stills with a sizeable chunk of Mom's deep-fried halibut on it. What is he doing here?

"What is *he* doing here?" Mark scoffs, and my lip twitches that we were thinking the exact same thing.

Guess that's to be expected when you've been friends since elementary school.

"Violet said something about talking with him on the flight to the lower forty-eight. Maybe she invited him?" I dab the halibut in Mom's homemade tartar sauce.

"Well, I wish she hadn't." Mark doesn't mask the anger in his voice at all.

He still hates Dax for how he treated me growing up. When I started going to Dax's gym, Mark couldn't believe I'd give "the pigheaded jerk"—Mark's words, not mine—a penny of my money. I wasn't too thrilled at first, either, but I liked the openness of Dax's place and that I could go at five in the morning and no one was there. Well, no one but Dax, that is. At least he hasn't been a bully like he was in school.

Besides, Dax's treatment of me probably had to do with childish compensation for some inner wound. I've learned all about those in my character development books and classes. He hasn't been mean since high school graduation. While he hasn't exactly talked much to me beyond grunts of, "Hey," and low-toned, "Need help?" in the mornings when we have his gym practically to ourselves, he isn't antagonistic.

I pause, remembering the gruff comments about working out my thumbs more than anything else. It's not a bad thing that I type my books on my phone while I'm on the treadmill. I'm trying to maximize my time.

I shrug, determined to be the mature adult, and nudge Mark with my shoulder. "If he starts hanging out with Kemp and Violet more, you might have to learn to play nice."

"Nope. Not gonna happen. Not after how he treated you." Mark stabs his halibut and shoves a large piece in his mouth.

What would I do without Mark? He's been my best

friend for as long as I can remember. Even though things have kind of gotten strained between us, I still can go to him when I need help.

Dax's gaze connects with mine, his eyes bouncing to Mark and back to me with a slight smirk. Dax veers toward us, and I silently beg Mark to behave. Not that Mark has ever done anything that could be considered confrontational, but he's been off lately, and I don't want to make a scene at Violet's party.

Dax stops a few feet away, glances at my plate full of potato salad and fried halibut, then lifts his eyebrow in silent condemnation. My eyelids slit into a glare. I know eating this will cancel any effort I put in at the gym this morning. Shoot, I'll probably wake up five pounds heavier, but it's a celebration.

"See you at the gym tomorrow?" Dax asks, and Mark freezes next to me.

No hello or even his normal grunted, "Hey." Just words oozing thick with doubt.

"Maybe," I snap.

He just huffs a laugh, shakes his head, and walks toward Violet and Kemp.

I take back him not being a bully.

Dax is a brute.

Always has been.

Always will be.

To pre-order Wild about Rory, *visit shop.sarablackard.com.*

Falling for my enemy? Nope. Not gonna happen. There's too many years of animosity between us to even entertain a relationship.

*Wild About Rory **is a laugh-out-loud, heart-melting opposites attract romcom with an*** *indoorsy romance author heroine, an adventure-loving hero, and swoonworthy chemistry that keeps you turning the page.*

indoorsy romance author heroine, an adventure-loving hero, and swoonworthy chemistry that keeps you turning the page.

Also by Sara Blackard

Vestige in Time Series

Vestige of Power

Vestige of Hope

Vestige of Legacy

Vestige of Courage

Stryker Security Force Series

Mission Out of Control

Falling For Zeke

Capturing Sosimo

Celebrating Tina

Crashing Into Jake

Discovering Rafe

Convincing Derrick

Honoring Lena

Alaskan Rebels Series

A Rebel's Heart

A Rebel's Beacon

A Rebel's Promise

A Rebel's Trust

Wild Hearts of Alaska

Wild about Denali

Wild about Violet

Wild about Rory

<u>Other Books</u>

Meeting Up with the Consultant

About the Author

Sara Blackard is an award-winning romance novelist who writes stories that thrill the imagination and strum heartstrings. When she's not crafting wild adventures and romances that make readers swoon, she's home-schooling her four adventurous boys and one fearless princess, keeping their off-grid house running (don't ask if it's clean), or enjoying the Alaskan lifestyle she and her Hunky Hubster love. Visit her website at shop. sarablackard.com